THE ODIA STORY
(Fifteen classic Odia short stories in translation)

THE ODIA STORY
(Fifteen classic Odia short stories in translation)

- Fakir Mohan Senapati
- Gopinath Mohanty
- Surendra Mohanty
- Kishori Charan Das
- Achyutananda Pati
- Mohapatra Nilamani Sahoo
- Akhila Mohan Pattnaik
- Chandrasekhar Rath
- Manoj Das
- Rabi Pattanayak
- Binapani Mohanty
- Pratibha Ray
- Ramachandra Behera
- Tarun Kanti Mishra
- Gourahari Das

Translated and edited by
Dr. Manoranjan Mishra

BLACK EAGLE BOOKS
Dublin, USA | Bhubaneswar, India

Black Eagle Books
USA address:
7464 Wisdom Lane
Dublin, OH 43016

India address:
E/312, Trident Galaxy, Kalinga Nagar,
Bhubaneswar-751003, Odisha, India

E-mail: info@blackeaglebooks.org
Website: www.blackeaglebooks.org

First International Edition Published by
Black Eagle Books, 2023

THE ODIA STORY
(Fifteen classic Odia short stories in translation)
by **Eminent Odia Writers**

Translated by **Dr. Manoranjan Mishra**

Original Copyright © **Original Authors**
Translation Copyright © **Dr. Manoranjan Mishra**

Cover & Interior Design: Ezy's Publication

ISBN- 978-1-64560-464-8 (Paperback)
Library of Congress Control Number: 2023948122

Printed in the United States of America

Contents

Introduction

Dear Readers,

We present before you a platter full of delightful and enchanting Odia stories, written by past and present masters, translated into English. We start with the 'Father of Odia nationalism and Odia Short Stories', Fakir Mohan Senapati, who is believed to have laid the foundation of Odia short stories with his 'Rebati' in 1898. Fifteen stories have been included in this anthology. Most of the writers included here were either born in the first half of the twentieth century or shot to prominence during that period. Among the writers Fakir Mohan Senapati, Gopinath Mohanty, Surendra Mohanty, Kishori Charan Das, Achyutananda Pati, Mohapatra Nilamani Sahoo, Akhila Mohan Pattnaik, Chandrasekhar Rath, Manoj Das, Rabi Pattanayak, Binapani Mohanty, Pratibha Ray and Ramachandra Behera were born in the pre-independent India whereas Tarun Kanti Mishra and Gourahari Das were born after India attained independence. Together, these masters have been awarded with twelve Central Sahitya Akademi awards, eleven Odisha Sahitya Akademi awards, seven Sarala Puraskars, five Atibadi Jagannath Das awards, two Jnanapitha awards and one Moortidevi award. Besides, the list includes four Padma Shri and two Padma Bhusan awards. The numerous awards reflect their excellence in the field of Odia literature and their invaluable contribution to it.

Fakir Mohan Senapati's story "Dhuliababa" reflects how the poor, gullible people were exploited by the so-called miracle performing mahants. The writer's attempt for social reformation, by exposing the real character of the mahants, is delineated here. Contrary to the previous mahants, who were blessed with divine qualities, the present incumbent Baander Das Mahant Maharaj contrives ingenious ways to deceive the locals. "His body looked as if smeared with a layer of dust." This was what lent him his local name—Dhuliababa, the saint covered with dust. He always thought of ways to squeeze some money out of the disciples. He would call up both the complainant and the defendant in case of a dispute, bless them, and make them promise to part with a fixed sum of money in case of success. Wouldn't one of them become successful? Once he announced that Fire-God would appear before them and fulfill their desires. Anyone can participate in the puja by offering certain donations. The local people participated enthusiastically in the proceedings. In order to deceive them, Dhuliababa had got a tunnel dug from the nearby room to the place of the fire and made one of the disciples sit inside and answer the questions of the public. Finally, Dhuliababa and his disciple fall into the hollow and burn themselves in to ashes in the same fire. Fakir Mohan establishes that evil cannot last long. One day or the other truth will come to light.

Gopinath Mohanty is not far behind. If it was the mahant who exploited the gullible people in Fakir Mohan's story, it was a so-called god-incarnate who exploited others in his story "Strange Faith". The innocent young narrator in the story finds himself crushed between the foolish faith of his village elders on one hand and the reasoning of a rational uncle on the other. The villagers of Gotama and surrounding villages believe that Lord Krishna has taken an incarnation in Gotama and soon all their worries will disappear. They believe in the antics of Batia and a group of his fanatic followers. Nilu uncle argues, "Jara Shabara killed Lord Krishna with his arrow. Life went out of his body. so, the body was cremated…(his) 'soul' might enter another body but his physical appearance completely changes" but to no avail. However, truth is revealed at the end. People realize that Batia is no incarnation of the Lord but another ordinary human being like them. The story ends with a lesson. "So long as you run after wealth and prosperity without making yourselves worthy, people will exploit you and try to take advantage of you. Batia might have fled but Hatia would soon replace him."

Surendra Mohanty's "Cactus" establishes that despite aloneness, aloofness, despondencies, uncertainties, and a sense of void enveloping life, life needs to be viewed positively and is to be lived accordingly. Since the tourist season had not begun, only a few guests visited Hotel Golden Beach. Among the occupants were Mrs. and Mr. Bailie and Mantu Mohapatra. Later they were joined by Mr. N. Mathur and Mrs. Rajan. In contrast to the aloofness and languor that spread in the hotel and its surrounding, the Bailie couple seemed to be living a life of their own. In the afternoons the couple would visit the seashore. "Mr. Bailie would sit almost in the same posture at the same place while Mrs. Bailie would roam around the beach collecting oyster shells. After some time, Mrs. Bailie, like a restless jovial girl, would proudly pour her collections before Mr. Bailie and rest her tired limbs beside him. Mr. Bailie would collect and stash those into his brown Bermuda pockets." Their behaviour surprises Mantu. Were the Bailie couple trying to prove that they were 'self-indulgent' and 'complete by themselves'? The appearance of Mr. Mathur and Mrs. Rajan is surrounded by mystery. Both of them appear there by providing wrong information about their whereabouts to their spouses. The sense of detachment seems to have taken Mrs. Rajan in its wake. She starts behaving in a mysterious way with Mr. Mathur and later, with Mantu. Her sudden return from the hotel leaves the mystery unsolved.

"Shashwatee" by Kishori Charan Das startles the readers both at the beginning and at the end. The narrator, who is critical of Shashwatee's inappropriate behavior, accepts her for her consistency in maintaining inappropriateness and for being different from others. The very first line of the story startles the reader. "Doesn't my father's face resemble that of a monkey's?" Pareshnath, the narrator, paying Shashwatee a visit in London, is taken by surprise. How could a daughter foster such an opinion of her father? How can a lady be so impudent? Was she boastful simply because she was tall, young and charming? Back in India a little enquiry reveals that her remark about her father wasn't an act of 'ordinary impudence' or 'extraordinary childishness'. From her very childhood days, she was different. She had always made fun of his abnormal face, education, wisdom, and even, blood pressure. The reader is surprised once again towards the end. It was the same Shashwatee who had got married to a person who looked 'worse than a gorilla or a chimpanzee.' The narrator seems to have developed a liking for her towards the end of the story. He feels that she had married only because he was foolish and she wanted to have absolute control over him. "For her men should be half-wits so that she could use them as puppets."

Achyutananda Pati's "The Sulking Mounabati" is an attempt to bring to the fore the evils that are put under a veil so that a fake shining façade can be maintained. The revelation of the truth sheds new light on the meaning of existence. Mounabati, the sulking princess of Ranga Island, is adamant on not marrying any young man of her state as she is made to believe that in their world "evil permeated everywhere and venomous serpents spewed out their venom all around. There was no dearth of instances of falsehood, thievery, spitefulness and conflicts." If she goes outside the confines of the palace, she is sure to stain herself. The King announces that anyone who 'appeased the wrath' of the princess will get her. Many princes test their luck but fail to impress her. Finally, a young gardener working in the royal garden arrives. He narrates four tales to the princess. The princess is moved to hear the tales of atrocity and treachery. The young man passes the test, invites her to break the shackles, remove the veil that blinded her, venture outside the palace, and discover the truth of existence herself.

"The Final Offering at Vrindavan" by Mohapatra Nilamani Sahoo showcases the desperate attempts by a saint to serve the Lord after the villagers desert Him. His own inefficiencies as well as the apathy of villagers force him to take an extreme step. He gives up his life for the sake of the Lord. The deities of Radhakant Math of Kalyanpur village were once the owners of three hundred and sixty-two acres of landed property. After the death of the Mahant, the villagers took forceful possession of the landed property. They carried the old bricks even. They cut down the trees in the campus and carried the logs home. Chhota Babaji, the only saint left to take care of the lords, had to beg for alms to arrange bhog for the lords. When Radharani's silver crown and silver girdle were stolen, people alleged that the saint had stolen them. He persisted there thinking, "I'm the only one left to serve Him; if I leave Him, who'll take care of Him?" The apathy of the villagers compounded his trouble. When he realized that he would no more be able to arrange for the bhog of the lord, he along with the idols of the deities, jumped into the village pond. His dead body along with the images were fished out by the police two days later.

Akhila Mohan Pattanaik's "The Flower of the Fig Tree" is an account of a chance meeting that leads the protagonist to delve deep into a mother's love, her intense suffering on account of the daughter's absence and the stark reality that is sure to generate a sense of pathos. During a visit to Gouhati during one Puja vacation the narrator Ashok lives in a posh locality. One afternoon while he is on his way to the hotel, it suddenly starts raining. In order to prevent himself from getting drenched, he takes shelter in a house nearby. Moments later a car pulls up there and a lady emerges. She addresses him as Sanjay and ushers him inside. The 'excessive affection showered' by the lady prevents him from revealing that she is mistaken. The lady complains about Manju who has not paid her a visit even though the holidays are going to end and she is going to head for London soon thereafter. The next morning, the lady's husband visits the hotel and informs him that he shares astounding physical resemblance with Sanjay, who was to marry their daughter Manju but the marriage couldn't materialize. He requests the narrator to continue paying them visits and not to break the delusion of his wife. Later that day, the lady and her husband visit the narrator at the airport and hand him a packet for Manju. The packet has only Manju's name but no address. The lady's husband reveals that Manju died in a train accident a few years ago. The fact has not been revealed to the lady to prevent her mental condition from deteriorating further.

Chandrasekhar Rath's "The Neighbour" is an account of the conflicts in the mind of a suspicious protagonist on one hand and an overprotective, overzealous and humane unknown neighbour on the other. The narrator is transferred to a new place. He arrives at the place with his wife, children and belongings. Unfortunately, when they reach there, torrential rain welcomes them. Besides, the dark night adds to their trouble. To their good luck, they find Sadhu Behera, a watchman waiting for them. Ordered by his master, Sadhu makes all provisions for the narrator and his family. However, the city-bred narrator grows doubtful about his real intentions. He considers Sadhu the leader of a gang of dacoits, ready to pounce on them and loot them. This doubt makes the narrator suffer throughout the night. The story vividly describes how the conflict is resolved in the end.

"Bhola Grandpa and the Tiger" by Manoj Das presents some anecdotes related to Bhola Grandpa, a habitually forgetful old man. Through the characteristic touches of humour, the writer presents Bhola Grandpa. 'Bhola' in Odia means 'forgetful'. The story has one such forgetful person as its protagonist. The anecdotes related to his leaving his grandson in the fair ground, his lying on the narrator's verandah with his tongue stretched out, his strange dream, and his encounter with the Royal Bengal Tiger make the story an interesting read. The remark of his wife on the reasons of his death, "The old man must have forgotten to breathe." comes as an icing on the cake. The single sentence sums up the protagonist, Bhola Grandpa.

The Princess" by Rabi Pattnaik is an account of a princess who is proud of her pedigree and ancestry. No matter what happens, the sense of pride in her ancestry would never allow her to submit herself to a commoner. In a sudden turn of events, the narrator comes across Princess Ratnaprava Singhdeo, the princess of Rajagarh. The narrator and his wife grow friendship with the latter. Their friendship grows so intimate that the princess reveals the unfortunate events that had shattered her father first and then her mother. The couple is surprised to find a young and charming lady with a pleasing personality like her unmarried. The princess cites the absence of suitable princes as the reason. Finally, she receives an offer for marriage from Binod Kumar, I.A.S and Deputy Collector of the city. She spurns his offer with the following words: "The blood flowing through your veins is red in colour but the blood flowing through the veins of a princess like me is blue in colour. For such a person who has blue blood, every human being irrespective of whether he is powerful, wealthy or noble minded, is only but a commoner. How can a princess disrobe herself before a commoner and allow him to enjoy his body?"

Binapani Mohanty's "Courageous" has a protagonist who has just passed his matriculation examination. He craves for people who would understand his true feelings and allow him to live his life normally. Tipu, the protagonist, passes his matriculation examination in third division. Even some of his school mates who always fared poorly in school tests, far surpassed him in performance. From class there onwards, he had studied on scholarships and therefore his father hoped his name would figure among the top rankers and he would become an IAS officer. The debacle leaves his parents shattered. The accusations and insinuations hurt Tipu to the core and he thinks of leaving home forever or even, committing suicide. He wants a little sympathy, a little compassion. Unexpectedly, his friend Ladukeswar, the young man who had been arrested and sent to jail on charges of theft, displays some compassion and offers him food when he is hungry. Ladukeswar exposes the weakness in people like Tipu: "I know you rich men's children very well. You crumble very easily. You people believe in only one thing. Life must pass smoothly. If there's a small trouble, you would either commit suicide or leave home forever." The story compels parents to have a reorientation of their views regarding performance of their children in examinations.

Pratibha Ray's "The Banquet" is a satire of the wealthy people who lack compassion for the poor. Desire for sumptuous dishes, though from used plates, propels the young protagonist to work hard for the rich man, unasked. "Were children like him in any way better than worms in the gutter?", "While the dogs happily gobbled up the food, the children helplessly looked on.", "Why do they allow the aroma to be drifted away by the wind, tormenting the latter?", "Their dogs aren't served with the leftover food." "Poor children don't mind abuse." highlight the pathetic condition of the poor in general and the child in particular. The writer takes a dig at those who consider the poor 'worms in the gutter'. "If the wretched people or their soiled hands refuse to slog, who would clean the heaps of refuge or filth?" she asks. Through the mouth of the child-protagonist, the writer criticizes the rich. "The wealthy are generous in the sense that they never leave the plate clean." Don't the poor deserve a better treatment?

Ramachandra Behera's "Gopapura" is the story of a

father who fights against all odds to save his only child from an imminent death. The story also highlights government apathy, poverty and lack of adequate facilities on one hand, and hope, determination and continuous fight of people against all odds in order to survive. When Nirakar returns from his fields, he finds that his only child is sick. His wife Sumitra calls in the local doctor and administers medicine but there is no relief. The boy has hiccups and convulsions. Nirakar realizes that the child needs immediate medical attention. The problem is he has to cross a river to reach the other bank and travel up to the Headquarters Hospital. besides, the darkness of the night adds to his troubles. The couple soon reach the bank on their side for the boat service but find the boatman absent. On one hand, there is the question of the life and death of their only child and on the other, their inexperience in dealing with a swiftly flowing river. Despite odds heavily stacked against them, Nirakar decides to row the boat himself, much to the dismay of his wife. After hours of struggle and life-threatening experience, they reach the other bank. Nirakar's determination, daring and courage fetch the child from the jaws of death.

"Story of the Moonlit Night" by Tarun Kanti Mishra has a small child as its narrator. His keen sense of observation, innocent child-like questioning, the immense faith of his mother in Gods and his father's reaction to different episodes in life makes the story an interesting read. The family in the story has to face trouble as their business declines and there is little income. Besides, losing a court case adds to their troubles. Consequently, they have to disengage the cook, cut down on expenses, dispose of the old house, and shift to a new house. The protagonist, a tender-aged child, fails to comprehend the changes taking place and complains as any other child of his age would do. His elder sister, Pinky on the other hand, has a better understanding of the situation. She tries to make adjustments so that she doesn't cause additional trouble. The disintegration, the snapping of the bond that held them tied to this house, the gradual shattering of their dreams, and the consequential sorrow have got apt treatment by the writer.

"Decision" by Gourahari Das highlights the importance of relationships and memories in the life of man. Money can never be a substitute for one's fond memories. Sulochana accuses her husband of apathy and indecision as he fails to sale off the paternal property of his share in his native village. The sale proceeds could have helped their only son fulfil his dream of building a house in Bhubaneswar. Besides, why should the brother-in-law's family enjoy the benefits? After the death of her husband, Sulochana proceeds to Patapur with her son, daughter-in-law and grandson to finalize the sale. They had contacted some prospective buyers while at Bhubaneswar. Sulochana undergoes a transformation after living for a day in the village. "Memory of the last fifty years lay embedded on the walls of the house…wherever she looked, she found the incidents related to her past life painted with bright, bold strokes." The memories cling to her and haunt her. She now understands why her husband had not been able to dispose of the property. She comes to the conclusion that he had taken the 'best decision' in not taking any decision at all.

I am sure you all will relish the stories.

- Manoranjan Mishra

Dhulia Baba

Fakir Mohan Senapati

Lord Hanuman of Degaon was famed all around for being a benevolent God. He wasn't a God of the *kaliyug*; He had been reigning since the *satyayug*. The *mahant*, Hanuman Das Maharaj, was no less famed. A pious person, whatever he ordered one, would materialize in no time. The entire state knew more of less of his strange powers. Once a Maratha army officer, on getting to know about his divine powers, rushed to meet him. It was early in the morning. The *mahant* was sitting on his wooden-seat and packing his chillum with cannabis to puff. He marked from a distance that the army officer, sitting on a huge tusked elephant and boastfully enjoying in the shade of a silk-umbrella, was coming towards him. The *mahant* only ordered, "Move... my dear wooden-seat...move." How could the wooden-seat disobey the *mahant*? It moved towards the elephant. The incredible sight was enough to teach the proud officer a lesson. He immediately jumped off his seat and prostrated at the feet of the *mahant* seeking to be pardoned. The *mahant* blessed him, "Let you live long...son...get up...get up." The moment the officer got up, he ordered that twelve *batis* of land be recorded in the name of the *mahant* immediately and the deed be inscribed on a copper plate. This *mahant* was enthroned for a period of twelve hundred twelve months and twelve days. Once a disturbing thought came to his mind. His stay on the earth had been considerably delayed for various reasons. He should bid it goodbye sooner. Enough was enough. This message was sent to Ayodhya. Another disciple was called for. The moment he arrived, the former *mahant* enthroned the new *mahant* and left for his heavenly abode.

The new *mahant*'s name was Markat Das Mahant Maharaj, well in sync with the sect that he belonged to. During his reign, the responsibility of collecting tax fell in the hands of the British officers. The officer at Cuttack said, "What? How come the Hindu *mahant* is enjoying benefits from so much land without paying a single penny as tax! Summon him. I'll examine the matter." On receiving the summon, the *mahant* started off on horseback. Flags kept flying at the head of the procession. His disciples joined the procession in large numbers. Some of them shouted 'Haribol'; some others performed *kirtan* and sang bhajans in praise of the lord. The *mahant* and his troupe reached the banks of river Mahanadi. It was a day in the month of *Bhadrab*. River Mahanadi was full to the brim as it was in spate. A storm was gathering just then. The boatman was reluctant to ferry them across. How would they cross the river now? The *mahant* said, "Don't worry; we'll cross the river soon." He pulled out a tiger-skin that he had tucked under his arm, spread it on the water and clambered onto it. He also took his officers, menial servants and cook with him. A flag-bearer held a silken umbrella over his head. He also had two people to steer the skin like a boat. On the other bank sat the British officer in a tent. He noticed the spectacle through his binoculars and asked another officer sitting nearby, "What's that?" The officer reported that a Hindu *mahant* was coming across the river to meet him. How could the officer continue sitting in his chair after all this? He ran to the river bank. He took off his hat and saluted him three times. He said, "Hello, *mahant*. The rent-free status on your land is restored forthwith." This *mahant* was enthroned for a period of one and a half thousand years.

After him, was enthroned, Jambuban Mahant Maharaj. Do you know the story behind the bi-forked *sahada* tree at the back of the temple? One day, the *mahant* was brushing his teeth with a brush made of a slender *sahada* branch. After he had brushed his teeth, he split the piece into two and scraped his tongue. After that, he joined both parts and stuck them into the soil. The moment he sprinkled a little water on them, they sprouted. They have now grown to a full-fledged tree.

The incumbent *mahant* is Baander Das Mahant Maharaj. A rare breed. He is five-hands tall; his chubby cheeks and lips touch his chest. His neck is hardly visible. His arms are as muscular as people's thighs. His tummy resembles an earthen pot fit to contain some stuff measuring ten-*nautis*. People without much acquaintance with him might accuse him of being nude but this is not an apt description of him. He usually puts on a one-hand span wide, one and a half hand-span long loin-cloth. However, the loin-cloth remains invisible as the thighs touch each other and the huge tummy hangs loose over it. This *mahant* is equally famed like his predecessors.

The temple had many beds but he would never sleep on them. Most of the time, he preferred lying on the ground, smearing himself with dust. His body looked as if smeared with a layer of dust. He never bathed; he hardly drank water. This was precisely why people addressed him 'Dhulia Baba'. The temple possessed unaccountable wealth; a great variety of cakes and sweets were prepared for the worship of the deities; he would hardly touch anything. Every day ten *seers* of unadulterated milk was procured; it was boiled long so that five *seers* of it was left in the end. It would also have a thick layer of cream, of the color of lac-dye, on the top. This was offered as *bhog* to the gods in the afternoon. The *mahant* would happily swallow only this. Besides, he would consume a *tola* of opium and a quarter of cannabis. Any time during the day and night, one would surely find the chillum in his hand. The two eyes looked red like vermilion. He would look at others with half-shut eyes. The chillum that he carried was almost a hand long. He would always be surrounded by a group of ten to fifteen disciples. It was the responsibility of five of them to keep the chillum filled with cannabis. After feeding themselves with Prasad in the temple, they would always give company to the *mahant*.

Everybody who came under the jurisdiction of the former *mahants* knew pretty well how glorious they were. Their glorious actions, written on the bark of birch trees in red colour, were secretly placed under the seat of the *mahant*. Dhulia Baba would read those secret documents and divulge the secrets only before close confidants. "Some thoughtless, imprudent traitor might reveal the secrets to others," he feared.

Dhulia Baba would tell his disciples every day, "When the Jagannath temple of Puri was consecrated, one thousand and eight sadhus and *mahants* came from Ayodhya to participate in the festivities. He was among them. Unable to evade the love and affection of the disciples, he decided to stay back. But, he had grown tired of the growing deceit and treachery; he would soon return to Ayodhya." The disciples would prostrate on the ground at his feet and beseech him to reconsider his decision. Out of pity for these disciples, Dhulia Baba couldn't desert them. This has recurred hundreds of times.

The *mahant* was the owner of immense wealth. He owned herds of cows and buffaloes. The amount of rice and money that he collected was measureless. One special way of earning money was this: when there was a dispute between two parties, both the complainant and the defendant would visit him in turns. Each of them would pray for his success and promise an amount in case the judge ruled in his favour. The record-keeper would keep a record of the promised amount. A disciple would be sent to the person who had got the degree and the promised sum would be collected from him.

Ram Sahu and Shyam Sahu were brothers. As dispute arose between them with regard to division of parental property, a civil case was filed in the High Court at Cuttack. Ram Sahu paid a visit to the *mahant*, sought his blessings and promised to pay a certain sum if the case went in his favor. The promised amount was recorded by the record-keeper. On the other hand, Shyam Sahu gave the *mahant* a miss. So, a disciple was sent to enquire why he had failed to show up. The disciple returned and informed the *mahant*, "My lord! I am afraid of saying what I heard. How adamant Shyam has become! In front of some villagers he was heard saying, 'This is *kaliyug*. The *mahant* has lost his charisma. Why should I go to him seeking his blessings when he himself has lost his charm?" The *mahant* was puffing cannabis then. Flying into a rage, he puffed with so much force that the cannabis in the chillum at once caught fire. The *mahant* puffed out smoke and said in a whispering voice, "My dear disciples. I'll now issue a proclamation. The fire in the chillum will do the speaking."

The joys of the disciples knew no bounds. They were firm in their conviction that the orders of Dhulia Baba could never be repudiated. In a single day, the rumour spread like wild fire across the length and breadth of the state: "God appeared in Dhulia Baba's dreams. He has granted him sainthood. His chillum will do the talking." Some other disciples said, "No...no...not the chillum but the fire in the chillum will do the talking." When ten people themselves bore witness to the order, who could question the veracity of the claim? A crowd gathered in front of Baba's abode for favorable orders.

The perennially ill people wanted a cure for their diseases. Those whose bullocks were missing wanted the Baba to provide some clues about their whereabouts. Some others wanted degrees in the law-suits they had filed in courts. Many women had sent their humble offerings beseeching the chillum-God to bless them with sons. Still some others placed their offerings (four-*anna* coins) at the feet of the *mahant* and prostrated before him.

The *mahant* said, "Get up...get up...my dear children. I won't do any talking. The spark of fire that you see in my chillum will be used to ignite the pious sacrificial fire. Once appeased, the Fire-God will appear there. He'll hear everybody's prayer and grant boons accordingly. On the *Magha Purnami* day, the Fire-God will descend from heaven and roam around the Earth. He has ordered me in dream; I'll keep the pious, sacrificial fire burning till that day. That day, people can come here with their problems. The wishes of those who offer puja and pray him after making some donations will be fulfilled instantaneously."

The *mahant* prescribed the precepts of the puja. Oblations will be offered one hundred and eight times. Those who wished to participate in the puja could make the following donations: a brand new item of clothing, five-quarter measure of ghee, *bhog* of five different colors, flowers of five different colors. Besides, one had to deposit fee for the preceptor according to one's ability, but that should never be less than five twenty-five coins.

The puja of the pious, sacrificial fire started towards midnight on the *Magha Purnami* day. As soon as the *mahant* offered oblations, the Fire-God appeared. The fire started burning brightly. The moment someone prayed with folded hands and conveyed his troubles, the Fire-God would prescribe solutions, in a solemn voice, "Yes…no…done." When the whole thing was happening in front of people's eyes, where was the question of harboring a doubt? People stood dumbfounded at the spectacle; they rolled about on the ground in reverence. The atmosphere of the *math* reverberated with the shouts of '*Haribol*'.

When Shyam Sahu learnt about the developments, he lapsed into deep distress. He heard that people, on offering worship, were being granted boons. He thought if his brother was blessed with boons, it would mean havoc for him. The disputed property was worth lakhs. Rama would be awarded a degree in the case and he would take possession of everything. The angry *mahant* had ordered, "The *teli* boy must be taken to task and taught a lesson". Shyama lost his sense, unable to decide how to deal with the crisis. Lost in such distressing thoughts, he suddenly embarked upon a possible solution. He contacted the *mahunt*'s disciples, who were addicted to cannabis. He bribed then with ten-rupee notes, fell at their feet and sought their intervention. They all advised him to prostrate at the feet of the *mahant* and seek to be pardoned.

It was about noon. The *mahant* sat on the ground with his disciples surrounding him. He was puffing cannabis; the smoke permeated all around. Shyam reached the spot, his chest pounding heavily. He flung a handful of jingling coins at the feet of the *mahant* and lay prostrate there. He stammered an apology, "O Lord, my mistake was the result of my child-like innocence. I am a sinner. I beg to be pardoned." The *mahant* continued puffing cannabis, with his eyes closed; he passed no orders. All at once the other disciples present there prostrated at his feet and prayed, "O, Lord. We are sinners, criminals. If you don't grant us pardon, who else will?" The benevolent *mahant* softened. He ordered at once, "Go, child…go. Arrange for the puja."

Shyam Sahu's joys knew no bounds. He ran here and there making arrangements for the *puja*. He was an affluent businessman; the arrangements must be grand in sync with his status. In place of the five quarter ghee that others brought, he arranged five *seer*s of it. Other items required for the *puja* were also procured in sufficient quantities. People usually brought cotton sarees for oblation. Shyama Sahu procured a Berhampur-silk saree with lace border and the figures of pitchers hand-woven on it. People came to know that a huge *puja* would be organized for Shyama Sahu. Both the brothers were rich businessmen. People from five villages around flocked the *math* to hear what boon was going to be granted by the Fire-God. Around five hundred people had already assembled on the temple premises. There was hardly any space left.

In the temple precincts, a row of houses had been constructed adjacent to the boundary wall. During fairs and celebrations, one of those was used to prepare cakes and sweets for the gods. The room next to it was the store-room. The ceremonial fire was kept burning in the room where cakes and sweets were prepared for the Gods. At about midnight, the *mahant* emerged from an inner chamber. He seemed to be in an ecstatic state. In anticipation of a handsome income, he had consumed an extra doze of opium in addition to the normal doze. Besides, he had smoked an adequate quantity of cannabis. His feet wobbled when he walked. He had to be carried by four disciples. The moment he appeared on the scene, all the devotees shouted '*Haribol*' and fell at his feet. The much-awaited *puja* began. Five-seer ghee was to be used in the oblation. The disciples placed a number of heavy logs on the fire. When the ghee was poured into the fire, it burnt four-hands high. Only the *mahant* sat in front of the fire. Only a pious soul like him could sit so close to the fire; could anyone else even enter the room?

Shyam Sahu stood outside the room, near the threshold and prayed reverentially to the ceremonial fire with folded hands. The *mahant* closed his eyes and started praying in a loud voice, "O Fire-God, please grant a boon to Shyama...grant...grant...grant. Let the verdict in the court-case go in his favor." The Fire-God didn't answer. In order to display his power to the people, the *mahant* stood up. With the ten-*seer* iron forceps that he was holding in his hand, he banged into the fire very heavily. Suddenly, a loud sound was heard. Shyam Sahu was startled. He looked inside to find a pit, chest high. The pit was half-filled with the burning logs. Two people were found inside the pit, as if lost in a wrestling bout. Initially, Shyam couldn't understand what was going on. But a little later, by virtue of his devotion, he understood that the Fire-God had taken the form of a human being and was locked in an embrace with the *mahant*. He was very fortunate; he was going to be blessed with boons soon. He himself shouted '*Haribol*' loudly and informed the gathering that the Fire-god had taken the form of a human being. The crowd started shouting '*Haribol*' in ecstasy. Gongs, cymbals, and trumpets were sounded. The sounds that emanated from there resembled the roar of the sea. The crowd rushed forward to have a *darshan* of Fire-God. There was only one entrance to the room; besides, the room was filled with smoke. There was a stampede-like situation and many people received bodily injuries in the melee.

Three hours passed. The expectant people had already grown tired of chanting '*Haribol*'. Suddenly, the pungent odor of burning-corpses reached them. People were forced to cover their noses with cloth. Some respectable people of the area went near the door, inspected thoroughly and declared, "The *mahant* has already been burnt to ashes." Some wicked people who had gathered there shouted, "The Fire-God has already gobbled up the *mahant*. He may rush out of the room and gobble up everyone else. Run... run...run." Hearing their shout, people started running helter skelter. Even the temple priest and their servants fled from the spot. In a matter of a few seconds, the premises of the huge temple stood empty. Only the crackle of burning-wood emanated and the pungent odor spread.

The Gopalpur government police station was situated at a distance of two and a half *kosh* from Degaon. The message was sent there in the morning. The police Inspector arrived with five or six armed footmen and eight to ten chowkidars. When the Inspector reached, he noticed that not a single human being was visible in the entire village, forget about people in the vicinity of the temple. The front doors of all the houses were barred. After the chowkidars coaxed and cajoled, some women responded from inside. Most of them were found saying, there is no male member at home. Some of them had gone to search for their missing cattle; some others had gone to their relatives' house. Even some had gone to attend a community feast. But most of them had gone to attend court cases at Cuttack. After a long search, the temple priest and some servants were found. When an enquiry was conducted, the Inspector came to know that a tunnel, wide enough for a man to pass, had been dug from the store-room to the room where the sacrificial fire was made. Just under the place where the pious fire was burnt, a pit measuring two and a half hand-spans each in length, breadth and width had been dug. Just under the fire, there was only a span-thick soil left. Using the tunnel, one of the disciples of the *mahant* would go till the place where the fire was burnt. When the *mahant* asked some question, he would answer from inside. On that fateful day, a cannabis-addicted-disciple named Hunda Das sat under the fire. The *mahant* had lost his senses under the impact of intoxicants. A heavy man as he was, when he banged heavily on the fire with the forceps, the soil caved in and the pieces of burning logs fell into the pit. The two people i.e., the *mahant* and his disciple Hunda Das were burnt alive. Since there was a heavy commotion outside, nobody heard their painful shouts.

The Inspector wrote the report and sent the two partially burnt dead bodies to the town hospital for post-mortem.

❑

(Original Odia: *Dhulia Baba*)

Strange Faith

Gopinath Mohanty

It was extremely surprising how Lord Krishna had decided to appear in our village Gotama in this *kaliyug*. No...no... not a stone sculpture but a real human being, claimed to be an incarnation of the lord, suddenly descended on it.

If one travels about a *kosh* from our village along the bank of the Timiri River, he would find a place straight ahead of an old simili tree, where the water is unfathomably deep. Once when a fisherman cast his net, something heavy got caught in it. It was an idol if Lord Krishna, chest-high, sculpted of stone. Some government officials soon came, fished the idol out of water and ran away with it to Delhi or Calcutta or Bhubaneswar or to an alien land, no one knows exactly where!

But the appearance of lord Krishna that I have mentioned here is different. A live human being, he boasted of all the characteristics that a godly figure usually possesses--dark complexion, chubby cheeks, attractive eyes that looked fabulous with the application of collyrium, curly hair, marvelously chiseled out limbs, and a fleshy body. I was only eight years of age then. An aunt of mine, Chemi's mother to be precise, pointed at him from a distance and whispered, "Burunda, look there, here comes lord Krishna. Fall at his feet in obeisance". And lord Krishna... how mesmerizingly he moved on the village road with his feet crossed in a special stance and a flute in hand! He played the flute all the while. My aunt further said, "Do you know what song the flute is playing? It's only singing the name of Radha". Baffled, when I turned to look at aunt, I saw two streams of tear flowing down her cheeks.

She continued, "It's piety through many generations that has resulted in God taking incarnation in an insignificant and obscure village like Gotama. Now all our wishes shall be fulfilled. The village is soon going to be transformed into heaven. The goddess of wealth, Lakshmi shall visit everybody's doors. Wants shall disappear. Whatever one demands shall be fulfilled forthwith."

With happiness writ large on my face I said, "I just asked for a boon."

"What did you ask for?"

"Our teacher beats us mercilessly at school. Let him go away from here."

Oh, what a fool I was! Let me ask for some other boon.

"I asked for something more."

"What did you ask for this time?"

"I asked for an abundant supply of dried mango-cakes."

My aunt said, "You are no doubt a fool. God has taken birth in our village. It'll soon become prosperous. There'll be an abundance of paddy, gold, sarees and clothes for everybody. The village lands shall bear two crops in place of the usual one. Neither floods nor droughts shall affect those. There'll be enough water for the moong crop. Barns of all the villagers shall overflow with food grains. Each villager shall possess herds of cattle. There'll be plenty of ghee, milk and cheese. The poor and beggarly will have a change of fortune. Deceit and debauchery will be things of the past. People will hardly look crestfallen; everybody will put on smiles and dance their time away. Disenchantment, disagreement and squabbles will completely disappear; with everybody lost in singing praises of the lord, who will have time for such meanness? The *satyayug* has dawned; lord Krishna has descended on our village." She continued, "O lord! You have a better understanding of the workings of the human mind. Please guide me. Without you, my existence means nothing." She lay prostrate on the ground while continuing to shed tears. I couldn't understand why she behaved like that. When I turned around, I saw many like her lying prostrate on the bare ground.

I heard Nilu Uncle, my father's elder brother, calling me. He had sunken cheeks, wrinkled skin on the forehead, small sunken eyes, and a small beaked nose. The nose made him look fearful. Twitching my ears with the tip of his fingers, he said, "Why are you roaming here and there, like a mad dog, in this fierce sun, without taking rest at home or sitting in some shade? Did you come out to see lord Krishna? Come with me...quick." He dragged me to the one-roomed house of his. He lived alone there and cooked dishes himself as there was no one to take care of him. He shouted angrily once again and said, "Tell me the truth or else I'll pluck your ears. Didn't you come to see Lord Krishna?"

"Aunt showed me the lord."

"Listen to me carefully, you fool. The man whom

you consider an incarnation of lord Krishna, is Batia. He is the son of Jati Swain. Jatia played the role of Ravan, the king of Lanka, in stage performances during Ramanavmi celebrations. He died long ago. His widow disappeared with her son after her husband's death. I know everything about this Batia. What a cheater, swindler and trickster! A deceiving and scheming fellow, it's his habit to ruin people by taking advantage of their innocence. An awful human being!

I didn't fully understand what exactly he was hinting at except that Batia was a bad man. It automatically came out of my mouth, "Why do you say so, uncle?"

"Son, Jara Shabar killed lord Krishna with an arrow. 'Life' went out of his body. So, that body was cremated. Of course, that had happened ages back. Among human beings, many saint-like people are found. They do the duty assigned to them; they help people in various ways. When the final moment comes, they depart. Are they reborn? Their 'soul' might enter another body but the physical appearance completely changes. This fellow, Batia, isn't lord Krishna. He is neither an incarnation of God nor a saintly figure. He's nothing but a liar, sinner, cheater and debaucher.

The fear that I bore in my heart for uncle silenced me although a volley of questions raised. With uncle's face and eyes contorted in anger, I dare not ask anything. He continued, "Batia has mesmerized the inhabitants of Gotama and established himself as their messiah. The number of his followers has increased manifold. He has proclaimed himself lord Krishna. His followers are presumed to have been born with some divine spark. They are licensed to move around in our village as well as in the neighboring villages causing nuisance. Nobody dares to raise so much as a finger towards them. If someone accuses Batia of some misdoing, he is threatened with dire consequences. Batia has declared that I'm his enemy, Kansa. He must be planning some evil. Batia wants that every villager should foster an unquestioned allegiance to him, like a servant to its master. He considers it his right to lord over others. It is as if he has succeeded a long line of zamindars. If someone grows inimical to him, he stands at the foot of a Kadamaba tree and pronounces, 'This man is a demon'. He has pronounced Haria the sweetmeat seller Bakasura, Pana's mother Putana, Bana Swain Arghasura and so on. Whatever he pronounces, others repeat after him. Let him do whatever he wants. I'm lying-in wait for an opportunity to expose him. He can never escape from my watchful eyes."

"There's something important I want to tell you. Listen carefully. You're but a small child; nobody would be suspicious about you. Whenever you are in Batia's vicinity, keep a close watch on him. Pass me information about his doings. Do you understand?"

"Okay, uncle."

Uncle allowed me to dine with him every day. Whatever *bhog* he offered to the gods at home, be those bananas, guavas or sweet balls of puffed rice, he would pass those to me in the end. He would fetch me berries, guavas, plantains or papaya plucked from trees in his backyard. It's true that I dreaded him but I also loved him. He would insist on taking me to the river for a bath. I would grow scared when he drowned me in water playfully, used wet sand to remove dirt from my back, and removed scabs from my wounds while cleaning them. He was the eldest person in the family and I held him in high esteem. Apart from my mother, he was the only person whom I loved to listen. I agreed to act as a spy for him. I was delighted that I was entrusted such a great responsibility.

To tell the truth, I was confounded. Whether the man under scanner was really Batia or lord Krishna? Had he appeared to ensure that we got what we wished for or to exploit us and fulfill his selfish desires? Did he wish to lord over the innocent and gullible villagers? Did he wish them to bow down at his feet the rest of their lives? Whose words should I go for—the words of Chemi's mother or that of my uncle?

Hoping that my mother would be able to solve the dilemma, I lay bare my heart to her. She placed a bowl of pulse-soup in front of me and said, "Son, it's already quite late since you had had some food. Drink it."

"It's okay but mother, tell me whether he's lord Krishna or Batia?"

Mother explained, "Son, unless I work in people's houses, it gets difficult to arrange our meals. I boil paddy, work on the husking pedal, winnow impurities, grind spices throughout the day. My only dream is that you should grow up, get educated and secure a job so that we can live in peace. How does it matter whether Batia is lord Krishna or not? Has Krishna ever told anybody that he could get enough food without slogging? People harbor different wishes. Chemi's mother is looking for a groom for Chemi. Saita's father has a shop; he wishes to earn more profits. Most people are not contented with what they have; they always wish to have more and more. They wish to grow rich in a night. Such people wish lord Krishna to descend on the earth and fulfill their wishes. I foster no such hope. My only hope is you should grow up and become a man. Your father left me alone in the middle of the life's journey. Why should I foster a hope that can never be fulfilled? There are people who want to win elections and become ministers; there are others who want to lord over others; there are also those who want to own buildings. Such people have excessive desires and therefore, they want help from the lord."

"In that case, he isn't lord Krishna; he is Batia. Don't you think so, mother?"

"Son, don't spoil your time in such matters. Who knows the truth of everything? If you make fun of Batia and someone hears you, he'll turn vengeful. The entire village is dancing to his tune. If he really possesses some divine powers, he'll burn us down to ashes. How does it matter what he is? On the other hand, there's no need of singing his praise considering him the real Krishna. If he turns out to be a commoner like us; if he turns out to be a deceitful cheater, we'll be subjected to deep disgrace along with him. If he is playing tricks with people, one day or the other the truth will see the light of the day. Where will he go then? How does it matter what happens to him then?"

"Oh, mother! Why do you confound me like this? Simply tell me if he's lord Krishna or not?"

"Son, God exists in everyone. He's there in you as much as He's in me. Like that, He's in him."

"What do you mean by 'like that'? You're deliberately trying a twist. Please tell me who he really is."

"I've already answered your queries. I don't really know who he is; I don't bother either. You needn't bother about him. Let him be what he is. Is there any dearth of work to bother about him the whole day?"

"Who is he?"

"Bang your head as much as you can. I don't care."

I understood; it was no more possible to elicit an answer from her.

Krishna lived in the spacious drawing room of Mathuri Sahu, a businessman. Sahu had a few wooden chests in that room. No one knew what they contained even though each one of them had four to five huge locks on it. Pictures of Gods adorned the walls. He had arranged a huge bed and provided cushions and pillows. Many garlands hung around the bed. An assortment of scents that of resin, camphor and flowers emanated from the room. Krishna sat on the cot. Devotees gathered in front of the house and performed *sankirtan*. A crowd had surrounded Krishna. He was offered cream, butter, fruits and sweets and glasses of deep-boiled thick milk to drink. He chewed betel cones and displayed a perennial smile. When someone came to meet him, he would immediately inform him what he was in the previous birth. He also quoted lines from the Bhagavad Gita to prove his point. All these helped him conquer over the visitors.

Mathuri Sahu was a businessman and money-lender. He owned acres and acres of landed property. People would mortgage their land and gold ornaments with him in exchange for money. He would charge an exorbitant rate of interest. He never allowed any concessions of any kind. He would not budge even if one banged his head at his feet. He was only concerned about the profits he made. I didn't have much idea about him. It's from there I came to learn that Mathuri Sahu wasn't a normal human being but was sage Narad in the previous birth. The old man sat cross-legged at the foot of the bed and uttered 'Krishna Krishna' with closed eyes.

Later people were found discussing among themselves that Panu Jena was 'Subal,' Nari Mohanty was 'Sudam,' and the tall, thin and emaciated brahmin Bishi was 'Sribatsa' in their previous births. At times, such incredible tales would emerge from that room and people would listen to those, nonplussed.

"Hello brother, have you heard? Kelu Ghadei was king Nanda in the previous birth!"

"Unbelievable! How could Kelu Ghadei be king Nanda? He owns only five acres of landed property but has twelve mouths to feed. Of course, he owns a milch cow. It might be giving him two-*chatank* measure of milk. He is a khandayat by caste!"

"What's so incredible in all this? He was king Nanda in the previous birth; he has taken birth as Kalu Ghadei in Gotama village in this birth. The lord himself told this. They recognized each other a moment ago; they locked themselves in an embrace and cried horrendously. The old man's wife died a couple of years ago. He soon broke into wailing, "My sweet child! Where has your mother gone?"

It was Arikshit Moharana who was discussing what he had heard with the villagers. He wiped his tears and went further,

"The lord says that even mother Yashoda lives somewhere among the villagers. Only she needs to be identified. Everything has gone topsy-turvy in this *kaliyug*. How could someone recognize another when he fails to recognize himself? All troubles stem from this. Even Gods have turned deaf and dumb as stones, preferring to sit still in rain and shine.

Do you know? Some valiant soldiers of the yore

have been reborn as girls and doing household chores like sweeping the floors or doing dishes or riding horses today. Similarly, some women have been reborn as men. The lord said, 'You will all see—my mother shall surely appear. Yashoda, my mother, shall search for me and reach my abode. Ah! How lovingly she fed me in the past! How carefully she nursed me! How she ungrudgingly put up with the troubles I caused!"

Do you know what happened just then? The old Kapili Jena arrived, supported by a staff in hand, searching his way and coughing all along. You all have seen what a valiant young man he was once! It was difficult to find another person who could match his strength and carry the palanquin with so much ease. When he dug soil, he would dig enough for three labourers. Disease and old age had made him feeble and shaky. During the Ramanavami celebrations, he would play 'Hanuman'. Have you seen a more valorous and heroic 'Hanuman'? He would break strong branches of the mango tree with his bare hand and arrive on the stage carrying it. That Kapili Jena had shrunk physically now; he resembled the staff that he carried.

Arakshit Moharana paused a while. He would often get emotional while talking about the problems of others. A hardworking person, one would always find him engrossed in some work.

He further said, "The moment the lord saw Kapili Jena, he jumped off the bed, hugged him and shouted, 'Here comes my mother Yashoda'. O mother! Please recognize me. Please recognize yourself. You are Yashoda and I am your loving son, Krishna. Pointing at Kelu Ghadei he said, "Look at him. Can you tell me who he is? He is my father, King Nanda".

Devotees played cymbals and mridanga outside. Their jingling noise reverberated in the atmosphere. People shouted 'Haribol'. Kelu Ghadei looked at Kapili Jena in eyes of wonder; Kapili Jena was seven years older than him.

They bought a piece of saree from Mathuri Sahu's family and draped Kapili Jena with it. They made him wear bangles; they smeared the parting on his forehead with vermilion. His bald head and gray moustache appeared strange. The female devotees ululated and paid obeisance. The old man hardly uttered a word. He looked here and there with flustered eyes. If you go there, you'll find Kelu Ghadei and Kapili Jena sitting in the room together.

I ran to the spot to verify the statements ofM aharana uncle. It was exactly as he had said. Kapili Jena's condition evoked laughter but I was too afraid to laugh. I returned from there, amazed and reported everything to uncle.

Krishna, with a heap of garlands adorning his neck, was taken around the village in a procession. His female devotees surrounded him. If someone put him on her lap and fed, someone else washed his mouth. Someone else collected the water that he threw out after rinsing his mouth in a bowl. All devotees present there took a drop of this each as the holy *'adharamrit'*. The female devotees were discussing that the lord had already identified his eight principal queens, all female friends including Lalita and Visakha. Radha was going to be identified very soon; only she hadn't appeared before the lord. Once she appeared and was identified, there would be *rasaleela, jhulanjatra* and so many other celebrations.

There was always a crowd beside Krishna. Male and female devotees jostled with each other to have a *darshan*. Some prostrated at his feet; some were seen showering their affection; some were found caressing him, fanning him, wiping his sweat, feeding with all kinds of delicacies etc. Platefuls of *bhog* were offered; the remnants were distributed among the devotees. The atmosphere reverberated with the sounds of drums, conch shells, singing of hymns and ululations.

Bewildered by the proceedings, I felt my head reel. I was certain that a miracle was going to happen. On many occasions in the past, I had experienced a desire causing a disturbance in me—the desire to fly. I would extend my arms and wave them like wings. I would take the name of the lord and say, "If you are really Krishna, you will make me fly like a bird. Let people look at me with wonderstruck eyes when I fly". I would jump thinking that I would very soon soar into the sky but in vain. I yearned for many such wishes to be fulfilled. There was no dearth of hope even though nothing miraculous happened to establish my faith.

It was late in the afternoon the next day and intensely hot. I was wandering alone. To roam around and spot a bird here and an iguana there was my favorite pastime. I always preferred to wander alone, with no obstructions hindering the exercise of my will. An army of frogs was swimming in the water in a pond. I decided to hurl stones at them. I was alone in the grove that was interspersed with abundant wild bushes and anthills. Suddenly I heard the noise of bursting of something. I looked around and saw someone standing under a mango tree. He smoked a *biri* and patted his tommy. When he had finished smoking the first one, he got another one from near his ears and put it in his mouth. He fetched a matchbox from near his waist and lighted it. My surprise knew no bounds when I realized he was the same person whom the villagers worshipped as

Krishna. How come Krishna was smoking a *biri*? He had selected this lonely place to pass stool. I found the answers to my query. My uncle was right—he wasn't Krishna but Batia. I ran towards the village feeling overjoyed at having made a discovery.

Uncle was still taking rest. The door of his room was closed. I knocked on the door once but paused thinking he might scold me for roaming in the sun.

My aunt, Chemi's mother, wasn't ready to buy my arguments. She said, "Burunda…you foolish little chap… how would you understand complex issues like incarnation of lord Krishna? He has taken incarnation as a human being and therefore, he was expected to do everything that human beings do. Wouldn't he pass stool simply because he is God? So many villagers smoke *biri*; what's wrong if he smokes a few? He is the creator of everything in this world; does *biri* fall out of the ambit of 'everything'? Hmm…what a foolish fellow you are!

Her words couldn't satisfy me. Consequently, there was no end to my curiosity. I kept a close watch on Krishna's activities and passed on relevant information to uncle. How electrifying the atmosphere of the village became those days! People were found ardently participating in *sankirtans*, singing of *bhajans*, reading of scriptures, chanting '*Haribol*' in unison etc. Some people even danced in groups, along with Krishna, to the accompaniment of songs and musical instruments. People celebrated by baking cakes. Some would go around the village in a procession with Krishna at the front. Even boats were used during the processions. People from nearby villages came flocking to our village. Everybody believed, "All the demons, irrespective of where they are, shall be annihilated; all wishes shall be fulfilled; there shall be an abundance of wealth and prosperity".

Uncle stood as the only stumbling block on the path of the celebrations. He would admonish others saying, "You all have lost your brains, indulged in boozing, discarded your wisdom, bequeathed your sense of responsibility and despoiled the name and fame of your forefathers. Your activities make one shameful. His temper would flare the moment his eyes fell on Krishna. He would charge him for all kinds of mischief. In response, he would only flash a smile and say, "Who else other than Kansasura would say something of this sort?" and depart hastily from the spot. Some of his devotees would rush at uncle threateningly with raised staffs and swords. They would abuse uncle saying, "You wicked Kansasura! Your doomsday is drawing near". Uncle would stand on the front verandah, with an axe in hand, and challenge them, "Dare you set a foot on my stairs, I won't hesitate to behead the one. Remember, this is my vow."

In the darkness of the night, some worried villagers would visit uncle hush-hush. They would condemn those responsible for disgracing the village and chide Batia for befooling the people. Uncle would angrily shot back, "You weak-kneed fools, don't try to act smart. To hell with your timidity!" They would place reasons for their helplessness and disperse.

Who could say how long this Krishnaleela, the antics of this Krishna, would have continued? Was I old enough to evaluate things or form opinions at that age? No. But, today I see everything clear like daylight. None other than our fellow villagers was responsible for what happened those days. In the heart of hearts, they were yearning for such a thing to happen. They had prepared themselves accordingly. When you are ready to be bamboozled, tricksters take advantage of you; when you are ready to accept impediments, they dot your way; when you are willing to be beaten, others don't lose the opportunity. Your mind and actions lead you to the mishap. But what worth do my thoughts have? I am not an astrologer; how could I say what lay in store for the entire village?

However, the Krishnaleela couldn't continue unabated because of one person, who dared stand up against it. In a loud voice, he would frequently announce, "This is falsehood, cheating, deception and treachery. This is unacceptable. This is immoral and sinful and therefore, shouldn't be tolerated".

Those days, I thought there was nothing unnatural on uncle's part to do what he was doing. Of course, I didn't have the mind to evaluate whether it was natural or otherwise. I didn't comprehend fully what the import of his statements was.

But when I look back today and evaluate, shivers run down my spine. How worthy those few sentences were! Our villagers were displaying a strange but profound faith in the god-incarnate. Even harboring contradictory thoughts was considered sacrilegious. Whether at a personal level or in a group, people were supposed to express their allegiance to him. It was as if someone had issued a proclamation ordering people not to utter anything in contrary. People lived under great trepidation. If they pronounced anything contradictory, they would be smacked on the head; darkness would pervade the rest of their lives. The supporters of this farce boasted of staffs, swords and collective strength. If someone dared to flare them up, they would soon raze everything to the ground. Besides, the god-incarnate, their savior, was already ready to incite them.

"You wicked Kansasura! Beware or we'll pluck out your tongue; burst open your chest; cut off your liver; take hold of your entrails and use them as sacred-threads."

"Listen, O street dogs! Just mind my words. Dare anyone of you venture onto my verandah, your severed head will lie on the ground."

I don't know where he derived so much courage from.

Uncle's wife had passed away years ago. He had two sons. One of them had fled from home some forty years ago. There's no news of him. The second son lived far away. He neither visited his father nor enquired after him. Uncle had inherited much property from his forefathers; he had added to that during his young days. After even spending enough money on his sons, he was left with six acres of land, which he let out on share-cropping. He cooked his own food. The money that he was left with, after meeting personal expenses, was spent in organizing *Ramnavami* celebrations, purchasing clothes for the Gods, and in procuring dresses, masks, beard, hair, drums and all other paraphernalia required for the drama troupe. His regular contributions made it possible to organize children's festivals, community feasts and *Dolapurnima* festivals. He would speak nonchalantly about life and death, "Does it really matter how long I live!" He had made friends with everyone including the young and the old. He would play the *mridanga* and dance to his heart's content. He would teach the young people how to play *pakhawaj* or *mridanga*. He hardly depended on others; he did everything himself.

Once a vulture made a nest in the deodar tree growing on the banks of the river. Uncle said, "A vulture's nest! Premonition of evil to the village! Drive it away." Young men started pelting stones but they could hardly reach the top. "Let's destroy the nest," he suggested. Such tender branches at such a great height! If someone fell from there he would surely die. And lo! With an axe attached to his loin-cloth, uncle climbed up the tree, destroyed the nest and came down.

Uncle was hardly worried about life… or even, death.

Some villagers issued veiled threats. I grew concerned and cried. While comforting me he said, "Don't cry, Burundi. The one who takes birth is sure to die one day; why should, then, one be afraid of death?"

The accomplices of Krishna sought his intervention, "O, Lord! How long do we have to put up with the rebellious Kansasura and his acts of treason? We know you are kind and compassionate but you have to destroy the evil in order to protect the noble souls. Use your conch, discus, club and lotus".

Someone objected, "No…no…my lord…don't destroy him that way. He'll attain salvation forthwith."

Someone else said, "Subject him to untold miseries before hurling him to hell".

One day when Krishna was going through the village in a procession, uncle shouted, "Hey…you, Batia! You cheat…you debaucher! How long will you continue with this farce of yours? God won't forgive you".

Krishna shot back angrily, "Devotees, listen. Within a period of ten days, this wicked Kansasura will be annihilated. His days are numbered. I curse him thus".

"Hell with your curse! I spit on you and your curse. If you have such powers, annihilate me now in front of others."

All eyes were now focused on uncle, sure that the curse of the lord will bear fruit immediately and uncle's head will burn into ashes. But Krishna said, "You insolent fool! I have tolerated enough of your insolence. There's no escape from my punishment now. On the tenth day from today, you are surely going to be annihilated".

Uncle said, "All of you present here, please lend your ears to me. Make a promise today. If I don't die on the tenth day, pee on this Batia's face".

A loud roar…issue of fresh threats…abusive words directed at uncle…finally the shouting of 'Haribol' in unison. Uncle whispered into my ears, "Remember what I had told you. Keep a watch on their activities. Report whatever you hear. They must be planning some evil. They might pluck guavas from my backyard, run away with bunches of plantain or set my house on fire. Be careful".

I roamed around and kept a watch on them. They were all busy repeating the threats. They were dead sure uncle was going to die. Some were eagerly watching him to find out if he had taken ill or not. Someone was found saying, "Does one require falling ill in order to die? He may die of snakebite, thunder strike or sudden vomiting of blood. How long does it really take a man to die?"

Uncle's daily routine had undergone no change. Be it the early morning bath or his worship of God for one hour each in the morning, afternoon or evening, he performed everything as usual. He would roam around the village and fearlessly discuss the affairs of the village. His indomitable courage surprised others.

"How courageous the old man is!"

"It's because he's the real Kansasura. Have you ever seen any let up in his insolence? He would rather die than surrender."

The tenth day dawned. The village was heavily crowded that day. The noise of *sankirtans* and threats issued by the followers of Krishna could be heard. Some people were found repeating, "The day has dawned. Kansasura shall be annihilated today".

Some others were found rushing at uncle's door threateningly and shouting, "Hey… you… Kansasura, get ready. Pay your last respects to Gods. Your curtain falls today."

My house was situated some distance away. My mother and other relations shed tears. Chemi's mother was found saying, "The lord has proclaimed him Kansa. That's okay but who gave him birth as Kansa? Who created him? The same God. Let's see what happens now". She also wept.

Night fell as usual. Uncle took his dinner and went to bed as usual.

A huge expectant crowd gathered in front of uncle's house the next morning. They were curious to find if the door would be opened at all.

Uncle woke up hearing the noise and emerged outside. People looked at him in surprise. Uncle shouted, "Where's that cheater, Batia? Why are you looking at me in eyes of wonder? Go and drag him by his hair. Ask him… why no harm has been done to me when ten days have passed.

Krishna had disappeared. He was no more found in

Mathuri Sahu's house. The bed was lying empty. He was nowhere to be seen.

The patients who had approached for miracle-cure discovered that their illness had worsened. The legs of the lame hadn't straightened. The dilapidated huts of the poor hadn't been transformed to bungalows. The devotees' wealth hadn't been multiplied; all their dreams remained unrealized. A groom was still to be selected for Chemi. People were condemning themselves as they had foolishly hoped that their association with him would bring about transformation in every sphere of their lives but nothing of that sort happened. There were a few who had spent a fortune to earn the favor of the lord. They had presented him money, gold ornaments, expensive clothes but they realized their blunder. There were others who had served the lord in 'other' ways but now they were ashamed of expressing those publicly. Certain activities of the lord were talked about in public; certain others had to be given a decent burial for not despoiling the name of the village. Everybody was found unanimous in their opinion, "It was not lord Krishna who had taken incarnation but it was Batia—a cheater, debaucher, thief, swindler and trickster. If they met him again, they would certainly teach him a lesson".

People understood where they had erred. They came to uncle and begged to be forgiven. Uncle fondly rebuked them and said, "It seems you all have learnt a lesson but has it made you wiser? Can anyone achieve anything worthwhile without hard work? If you don't work, who will supply food forever? Unless you cleanse your body, mind and village yourself, who else will do it? No matter how much you slog, can the unattainable be attained? Can anyone prosper without hard work? So long as you run after wealth and prosperity without making yourselves worthy, people will exploit you and try to take advantage of you. Batia might have fled, but Hatia would soon replace him."

All the villagers gathered in front of uncle's house that evening. Uncle had prepared an effigy with pieces of bamboo and ropes. He said, "Imagine, this one is Batia. Do whatever you wish to do with him".

❑

(Original Odia: *Biswas*)

The Cactus

Surendra Mohanty

Hotel Golden Beach…
        The off-season still continued.

There was still some time for the pleasure-seeking tourists to flock, like batches of colorful butterflies.

The lonely seashore, the Golden Beach hotel and the green velvety lawn in front of it lay in wait for them, anxious and impatient.

In the shade of the palm tree on the lawn, on a cane chair, sat an Englishman in brown bermudas and a white half-shirt. Most probably, he was reading a copy of last week's 'The Statesman'. Sitting on another chair beside him, an elderly lady was found knitting wool.

They were occupants of suite no. 37, Mr. and Mrs. W. A. Bailie.

Although the X-mas season was over long ago, the couple had decided to stay back, like festoons and flower decorations.

Mantu, leaning on the railing on the verandah in front of room no. 12, was looking at them with pointless blank eyes.

The sea was in its usual disturbed state. It seemed as if the foamy waves were ready to inundate the verandah of the hotel.

Mr. and Mrs. Bailie sat with their backs towards the sea. Mr. Bailie had the three-day old copy of 'The Statesman' whereas Mrs. Bailie had the wool-bundle in front of her. A seagull flew above them, inciting them to throw away the newspaper and the wool-bundle and to feel animated like the lusty waves but in vain.

Mr. and Mrs. Bailie sat with their backs towards the sea, the sky, the beach and the seagulls.

Mantu wandered purposelessly towards the reception counter. The receptionist sat at the counter with a copy of an old 'Life' magazine. She appeared still, indifferent and unresponsive like a 'still-life' portrait. The telephone fell from his hands on the desk bringing an abrupt end to all his thoughts.

In the key-rack, all name-plate brackets with brass chains were lying empty.

The holidaying season was still a few days away.

An unfathomable gloomy void spread all around and seemed to be gazing at the visitors from the empty brackets. Only a card placed in the bracket no. 37 had these words written on it—Mr. and Mrs. W. A. Bailie.

The bracket numbered twelve had Mantu's visiting card on it.

M. Mohapatra.

Sales Representative.

Hardinge and Cockborne, Hardware and Steel Manufacturers etc.

When he approached, the receptionist raised her head from the pages of the 'Life' magazine and greeted him, "Good afternoon, Sir."

Mantu replied, "Namaskar."

The receptionist concentrated on the magazine once again.

The wall clock struck four.

The receptionist became a little animated on hearing the noise of the clock. She then came to the portico and called out to the driver...

Driver! Driver!

In the station-wagon parked in the portico, the driver had fallen asleep, with his face on the steering wheel.

Responding to the receptionist's call he got up wiping his eyes and looked, through two palm trees, towards a portion of the blue sea and the sky.

The receptionist spoke in broken Hindi and passed necessary instructions to the driver. "Some guests are arriving by seven UP. Take the wagon to the station...train expected to reach at five thirty, on time."

The receptionist returned to the counter and to the magazine lying open on it. The sleepy-eyed driver, yawning viciously, drove the vehicle out of the portico.

The crest of the foamy waves and the wings of the seagulls were smeared with the amber of the setting sun.

Probably for the hundredth time, Mantu cast his wearied eyes on the conch-shells and oyster-shells lying in a showcase of the reception counter. He heaved a sigh of relief thinking that the arrival of the guests would bring the much-needed freshness, bringing an end to the engulfing aloofness. What if the newcomers arriving by the seven UP were no different from the Bailie couple, who sat with their backs turned towards the sea, sky and the seagulls, with old newspapers and bundles of wool giving them company!

After the initial enchantment was over, the lonely hotel on the deserted beach surrounded by tamarisk trees and *kia* bushes, was gradually turning unbearable for Mantu.

He had been granted three month's sabbaticals. There was no dearth of either time or money. Despite this, a strange aloofness surrounded him. Everything that was novel and exciting looked like the folded ends of old magazines. Mantu, feeling stifled, had packed his bag and baggage a few times, intending to leave the place and flee. But if this place was infested by a deserted aloofness, other places were horribly crowded. Irrespective of the choice he made, the moments of leisure were bound to be absolutely lonely, devoid of enthusiasm and weighed down by a void.

Mantu wished to collect the names and other information about the guests scheduled to arrive sometime later from the receptionist but he refrained from doing so thinking that this was against the norms of decency.

The afternoon sun went down and down the western horizon. The tamarisk jungle that stood not too far away from the hotel and that looked empty-hearted during the day appeared mysterious at the dusk. Mantu decided to spend some time in its lap.

The fishing boats of the *Nolias* lay on the beach with their hulls buried into the sand. Mr. Bailie sat on one such boat with his back turned towards the setting sun and smoked a pipe. Mrs. Bailie, donning a red gown, was busy collecting oyster shells from the beach. She seemed to have betrayed her age.

Mantu had observed the recurrence of the same scene on the beach over the last few days—Mr. Bailie would sit almost in the same posture at the same place while Mrs. Bailie would run around the beach collecting colorful oyster shells. After some time Mrs. Bailie, like a restless jovial girl, would proudly pour her collections before Mr. Bailie and rest her tired limbs beside him. Mr. Bailie would collect and stash those into his brown Bermuda pockets. He would lift her up in an embracing posture; he would hold her with his hand around her waist; and they would return to the hotel.

Mantu had neither the desire nor the patience to watch the antics of the couple today. A strong malice colored Mantu's disenchantment with the Bailie couple.

On some occasions in the past, Mantu had tried to overhear their conversation. Mr. Bailie addressed Mrs. Bailie 'Darling' whereas Mrs. Bailie addressed him as 'Willie' or as 'You naughty boy'.

Mantu didn't wish to play the spy today. Nor did he wish to analyze how at the age of sixty or more the Bailie couple shamelessly tried to prove that they were self-indulgent and complete by themselves.

Like restless waves, a strange disturbance shot through Mantu's heart.

In the fading light of the dusk, the lonely and deserted shore appeared like the frontiers of the world. A Nolia boy ran on the foam infested beach towards the *Nolia* colony not too far away.

The sun had already set.

The station wagon had returned to the portico. Some bags and suitcases still lay there to be carried to the rooms of the guests.

The fleshy back of the obese elderly gentleman, who leaned on the counter, looked awkward.

While collecting his key from the receptionist Mantu noticed that the guest would be around fifty years of age, though the smart clothings made him look younger. A red handkerchief hung out of one pocket of the terylene trousers extravagantly.

Mantu somehow felt that he was intentionally dilly-dallying while entering his name and address in the Visitors' Register.

The guest enquired, "The two-bed suite that you have allotted to us doesn't have any leaking taps or showers, does it?"

With his gaze fixed on the empty columns of the register, he was as if lost in some thoughts.

Someone played a gramophone record, at this odd hour, in the jukebox that was lying in the hotel lounge unused like an archaeological object. No one had any idea who did it.

The receptionist responded in a gentle voice, "If you have any objections to this suite, I can allot suite number 8 to you."

The guest was still confounded.

With his pen fixed on one column of the register, he asked, "Is the sea visible from the room?"

"Sir, it's obviously visible as the hotel is situated close to the beach."

"I can manage with any room but 'madam' has certain preferences. The sea must be visible through the windows."

The receptionist suggested, slightly irritated, "In that case, please go for suite number twenty- seven."

The telephone suddenly rang. While the receptionist was picking up the receiver, the guest said, "You can allot two adjacent single rooms then. But make sure that the sea is visible from there."

The receptionist looked at the guest in eyes of wonder and shouted 'Hello...Hello' into the receiver. A trunk call... shouted the receptionist...Mrs. Rajan...I'm sorry there is nobody by that name."

Suddenly, a lady was seen rushing from the lounge towards the counter. She said, "Please...please...that trunk call is for me."

The lines on the guest's cheerless face wrinkled. The frown that he cast on Mrs. Rajan reflected an intense envy and malice.

Mantu, waiting to receive the keys, stopped for some time at the counter.

Mrs. Rajan spoke into the receiver with a smile on her face, "Just now...not even ten minutes...not bad...you wish to come? No problem...what was I doing? Playing a record on the jukebox...standing by my side...Would you like to talk to him?"

In an anger-ridden and hurtful voice the guest said, "Who's that?"

Mrs. Rajan placed her right palm, like an ivory cover, on the mouthpiece and blurted out, "Dr. Sudhansu".

The annoyed guest turned away his face in contempt and derision and said, "How did he know that we would have reached the hotel by this time? You must have informed him in advance."

Sudhansu's words, eloquent and delightful, floated out through the receiver. Unexpectedly Mrs. Rajan brought an abrupt end to the conversation, bid goodbye, and placed the receiver down.

The guest now looked in the direction of Mrs. Rajan and said, "I think a double-bedded suite is perfectly fine for us. But if by chance Sudhansu arrives, then…"

Swinging like a bunch of tube-roses Mrs. Rajan said, "How silly of you! Don't they have single suites? How terrible your snores sound! They would drown the roar of the sea."

The guest, in the manner of reaching a conclusion, told the receptionist, "Two single suites please…adjacent ones…I was telling you just that."

The receptionist cast a gratifying look, first at Mrs. Rajan and then at the guest. She presented the register to the latter and said, "Suite number 16 and 17…please put your signatures here."

While the guest was writing his name and address, curious Mantu looked at the page from the corners of his eyes. The guest concentrated on his task.

N. Mathur, Bombay.

Mrs. Rajan in the meantime had taken out her compact make-up box from her vanity bag and was busy putting on make-up. Mr. Mathur looked in her direction and said, "Suite no. 18 is yours…write your name here."

Mrs. Rajan, continuing to look at her perked up visage in the mirror, said, "You complete the formalities, dear."

The receptionist disapprovingly said, "I'm sorry madam…this is not acceptable. How can he write the name when you are going to stay? Such things aren't permitted here. You have to write your name and address in your own hand."

Mrs. Rajan cast a glance at the receptionist. She appeared to have lost her fickleness and become terribly frightened. Feeling utterly helpless, she wrote her name and address and fled to the verandah.

It was as if a ghost ran after her.

When Mantu followed her to the verandah, he met Mr. and Mrs. Bailie on the way. They were heading towards the dining hall for dinner. They appeared in formal evening gowns. It was as if they had been personally invited by the queen to the dinner party. Unmindful of the doubts, worries and uncertainties that surrounded others, they appeared calm and certain.

The east wind, guided by some perplexing emotion, was smashing the windows of the hotel rooms. The foamy waves of the sea were eagerly trying to touch the blue sky.

In the surroundings spread an immeasurable indifference and disquiet.

After breakfast, Mantu moved aimlessly on the verandah examining the cactus plants in brass pots. Some distance away, sitting in the shade of a palm tree in the lawn, Mr. Bailie was playing chess all alone. Mrs. Bailie, while browsing through the pages of a book in her lap, had dozed off.

Mrs. Rajan or Mr. Mathur was nowhere to be seen. Mrs. Rajan hadn't even come to the dining hall or to the reception counter to collect her letters received by post.

The jukebox in the lounge had reverted to its former silent state. Mantu had waited for long just to have a glimpse of Mrs. Rajan. He had engaged himself in unnecessary conversations with the receptionist.

Mrs. Rajan wasn't astoundingly charming. She was neither too young nor old. She might be a widow or a divorcee! For Mantu such considerations were worthless. He only wondered when and how, unknown to him, some inner core of his being was enticed by a strange attraction for the enchantress. Mantu knew quite well she was an adulterous woman; otherwise, she wouldn't have decided to visit a deserted sea-side hotel with her boy-friend like this. Besides, she had numerous calls coming from her other boy-friends from distant places.

Mrs. Rajan, like a colorful butterfly, flew around the life's garden entrapping the appreciators of her beauty. She could be an incarnation of a liberated woman from a noble family in the metros; she could be the provider of satiety in a society that craved for sensual gratification.

In the hearts of people like Mantu, who were always busy in the mundane affairs of the world, there was no space for stirrings of this self-destroying love. Like the cooing of the cuckoo filling the surroundings with a delightful music towards the fag end of spring, Mrs. Rajan had created a surprising stir in grown-up Mantu's inner being. Despite subjecting himself to intense self-examination, Mantu failed to comprehend how she could do it. They had spent but a few brief moments together during the last two or three days. Surprisingly, her charm enveloped his entire being completely.

Mantu was still lost in thoughts of her. He was frequently looking at Mrs. Rajan's door with expectant eyes.

Who knew what had happened to Mrs. Rajan?

It was a usually unremarkable evening two days ago. Mr. Bailie was sitting on a boat, its hull sunk into the sand, with his back towards the setting sun. Mrs. Bailie was roaming around the beach and collecting colorful oyster shells. In the light of the setting sun, she looked like a nimble-footed young girl.

Sitting beside a sand-heap, Mantu was looking at the tamarisk jungle, situated not too far away, in a vacant and pensive mood. Some unexpressed emotions, without having found a vent for expression, had turned the evening sky behind the tamarisk jungle red in pain. Mantu had miserably failed to penetrate into the deep secrets. Had he succeeded in his efforts, his anxiety-ridden mind would have got some respite.

Mr. Mathur and Mrs. Rajan walked out of the hotel and sat some distance away from Mantu. Mrs. Rajan had donned a sea-colored saree. She was swaying in the sea-breeze like a bunch of colorful flowers. On the other hand, an obese Mr. Mathur felt breathless walking here and there on the sand, as his feet sank into it.

Mrs. Rajan sat on the moist sand with her tender feet towards the waves that kept on lashing the shore, spreading their foam on the beach. Mr. Mathur sat by her side there.

Mantu, sitting beside the sand-heap grew extremely anxious and excited to overhear their conversation.

Mr. Mathur took Mrs. Rajan's hands in his palms and said, "You look astounding, Lily!"

Oh, Mrs. Rajan was named Lily! What's the harm if she were called Lila instead?

Lily or Lila remained mum.

Mr. Mathur said, "Ah! Please say something. Ever since we reached here you have suddenly grown morose. What was the need of coming so far, then?"

Lily or Lila responded in a choked voice, "The simple reason is you have your wife in Bombay, so you have come in pretext of going to Delhi on business; my husband is in Bombay, I have come here on pretext of meeting a friend of mine at Madras."

Mr. Mathur took Lily or Lila's hands in his own and spoke affectionately, "Does someone spoil such rare moments of freedom from life, feeling glum like this? Come...let's enjoy."

The way Mr. Mathur dragged Lily or Lila towards his lap, Mantu felt a deep jealousy overwhelming him. He thought of jumping out of where he was sitting, and announcing their debauchery to the whole world loudly.

Lila or Lily exploded unexpectedly and said, "Ah! Won't you allow me a moment's peace? You...good boy...go away from here. Go back to the hotel. Once I feel becalmed, I'll return to you."

Mr. Mathur's lips quivered. He was about to say something when Lila or Lily interrupted, "Please leave... why are you still sitting?"

Soon thereafter, without any provocation, she started throwing palmfuls of moist sand at Mr. Mathur like an enraged maiden. Mr. Mathur was left with no option other than fleeing from the spot.

A strange delight shot through Mantu's body.

Lila or Lily started taking a lonely stroll on the sea beach. By the time Mantu could hide himself, she was standing in front of him.

Finding Mantu near the sand heap, Lila shouted, "Hello...Good evening!"

Mantu wasn't ready for her greetings. In a confounded voice he responded, "Good evening".

Pointing at the tamarisk trees she said, "Have you ever entered the tamarisk jungle? I have been thinking of going there since the day I arrived here".

Surprising! Was she placing an indirect invitation before him to enter the tamarisk jungle in this resplendent dusk? But the way she had thrown palmfuls of moist sand at Mr. Mathur, dissuaded him from proceeding with his thoughts any further. The tufts of curly hair flew about her forehead. Mantu felt a twitching in his fingers to set that right. Keeping his desire in check, Mantu answered in a detached voice, "I've seen them from a distance only...I've never ventured inside."

He felt as if he was roaming in the dream world when he heard Lila or Lily say, "If you give me company, we can go there together; I am afraid of going there alone."

Mantu pinched himself a bit and from the pain and sensation gathered he wasn't in a dream world but was confronting the reality.

Lila or lily said, "Please come with me… see how the pale moon has started raising her head from the other side of the tamarisk jungle".

Mantu turned to see the bright moon raising its head from behind the tamarisk jungle to turn this mysterious evening more enigmatic.

The tamarisk jungle was still some distance away from them. Lila or Lily became tired of walking on the sand, as her feet would often sink in. At dusk the tamarisk jungle resembled a lonely dark night that lay helpless on the ground.

Lila or Lily collapsed to the sand and said, "We'll rather go there tomorrow. It's already dark here."

Mantu's desire had also waned by then. He sat down by her and lighted a cigarette.

Lila said, "Please give me a cigarette. I don't usually smoke outside but there's hardly anyone to object."

Something had turned Lila's face red—was it the excitement of an unsettled task or was it the fading glare of the setting sun?

Mantu opened the cigarette-case without hesitation and stretched out his hand towards Lila. While smelling the fragrance of expensive tobacco, Lila or Lily said, "These are 'Players,' aren't they? I also prefer this brand."

Mantu felt extremely grateful within. Lila or Lily couldn't light the cigarette despite striking a few matchsticks. She looked at him helplessly and said, "Why are you looking at me like this? Please light the cigarette".

Mantu's hands were quivering by then in an unexpected excitement. By the time he carried the lighted sticks near her lips, the breeze would extinguish those. Lila or Lily turned her cigarette and her lips towards Mantu and said, "Light mine with help of yours. It seems you are not much experienced in all this."

Of course, there was nothing much to laugh about but both Lila and Mantu burst out to a loud guffaw.

Lila, with her laugh, looked very much like the flying seagulls.

While Mantu's lips inched closer to that of Lila's, he could feel her warm breath on his cheeks. It seemed she was unnecessarily causing a delay in lighting the cigarette.

While puffing out a mouthful of smoke, Lila or Lily said, "You stay in room no 12, don't you?"

Mantu said, "How do you know?"

Lila or lily quipped, "What's so surprising in all this? There are just four guests in this big hotel. Where is the problem in finding out room numbers? Tell me what my room number is!"

Although Mantu had discovered the secret on the first night itself, he feigned ignorance and said, "Sorry, I don't know".

Lila or Lily threw a handful of sand on Mantu and said, "What a blatant lie! Why do you look at me with lustful eyes in the dining hall and at the reception counter then? Mr. Mathur believes you are completely uncivil."

The way Lila or Lily laughed, Mantu felt terribly confounded. A grown-up person as he was, his face turned red in disgrace. He felt as if he wasn't surrounded by a sea or the quicksand or the terrible roar of the waves and winds but as if he was flying in a vast limitless space.

Lila threw the cigarette butt after some time and said, "Let me go now. Please don't accompany me. I'm sure Mr. Mathur would be hiding somewhere nearby, waiting for me."

The mystery of the lonely evening was like a forbidden fruit confined to Lila and Mantu only. Nobody else had the right to trespass into it.

Mantu was surrounded by the restless sea, excited waves, distressing sighs of the tamarisk jungle and the upsetting cries of crazy winds.

Before Lila or Lily disappeared she turned back and said, "We'll surely explore the tamarisk jungle tomorrow".

After Lila had left, Mantu kept sitting on the sand, greatly overwhelmed by the events of the evening.

The next afternoon, much before sunset, Mantu was found sitting at the pre-fixed location, waiting for Lila or Lily. He was smoking one cigarette after another. He was rehearsing the witty dialogue that he was supposed to have with her on the way to the tamarisk jungle.

Had she forgotten about her promise? A few seagulls were encircling over the foamy waves. Rising out of the tamarisk jungle, the moon looked like a resplendent ball and like an incorporeal being in the lonely night's dream.

The tamarisk jungle surrounded by quicksand lay deserted.

Who knew what had happened to her? Was 'tomorrow evening' a pretention of that pretentious adulterous woman?

Such thoughts kept Mantu preoccupied. Each moment, he was inflicted with an intense pain.

Mantu discovered a bearer returning from room number sixteen with used bed-sheets and towels. He gathered courage and asked him, "What is Room no.16 madam doing?"

The bearer answered in a carefree manner, "She has already left since yesterday evening. The sahib living in room no. 17 is leaving today, in the evening."

The bearer cast a meaningful look on Mantu and left.

Mantu looked at the closed door of room no. 16 like a fool—like one who had been badly cheated.

Mr. Bailie had finished playing chess in the shade of the palm tree on the lawn. Mrs. Bailie was leaning on the chair and dozing like a helpless infant.

Mr. Bailie was waking her up gently and saying, "Come, darling…let's go".

The restless waves of the sea were frequently beating their heads on the beach looking for an assured support, a reliable shelter and an imperishable dream but in vain.

What was her real name- Lila or Lily?

What was her address?

Mantu heaved sighs of distress but continued brooding.

❑

(Original Odia: *Kaktus*)

Shashwatee

Kishori Charan Das

❙❙ Doesn't my father's face resemble that of a monkey's?"

How could a daughter, irrespective of how modern, independent-minded, free-willed and liberated she was, foster such an opinion about her father and that too, give vent to her feelings before one with whom she had no acquaintance before twenty-four hours? Pareshnath was startled to hear such remarks. He looked at the tall, perfectly chiseled lady sitting in front of her with wide eyes. If she had expressed that opinion in jest, he could have forgiven her but that wasn't the case. There was nothing in her demeanor that showed it was an off the cuff remark. A long-term cruelty reigned her aristocratic lips. Even after having made the remark, without being remorseful, she asked, "Do you appreciate my remark?" Pareshnath felt great anger seething in him. "What does the tall, slim lady think of herself? Doesn't she know the beauty and youth that she is proud of today are transitory?" He condemned and cursed her for her impudence. He could have left the place in a huff, but he found himself under obligation to carry out the orders of the monkey-faced man. He was his senior in the department. While bidding him good-bye before leaving for London, he heard the gentleman repeat: "Please meet Shashwatee and ask her how she is".

The gentleman was not only intelligent but also quick-witted. Even though he occupied the second position in terms of official hierarchy, he was like the highest authority. This was because the official who occupied the highest position was like the constitutional head of the country—a harmless, noble-minded person. Besides, he belonged to our part of the state. Pareshnath reminded himself that he was visiting Shashwatee as an emissary of her father. At the same time, he wanted to convey her that he reserved every right to be angry with her. He might be your father but he deserves my respect and truly so.

Pareshnath remembered that his Boss' letters resembled pearls. The files brought to him must be heaped neatly in the 'In' tray. As soon as he had finished working with them, he would tie the lace and put them in the 'out' tray neatly. The slightest disorder was unacceptable to him. If he needed to remove his spectacles, he would take it out gently and place it on the table, perfectly parallel to the surface. The handkerchief in his trouser pocket, the parting of hair and the iron-mark on his trousers—one had to see these to believe how careful he was about appearances. The most remarkable thing about him was his pronunciation. He would utter each syllable in a classical style. When he called out 'Pareshnath,' the palatal 'sh' was pronounced faultlessly. Even though his daughter's name required long pronunciation, he didn't cut it short. He would pronounce all the three letters, Sha-shwa-tee, with due stress on the palatal 'sh' and long 'ee'. How many officers were so aristocratic in their manners?

He had told him, "Pareshnath, please meet Shashwatee and ask her…"

Pareshnath tried to remind himself of what his boss had exactly told him. He felt proud that his boss had entrusted the responsibility to him. To think that there was something monkeyish in his behavior...this very thought was repulsive. He condemned himself for entertaining that thought even for a moment. Every part of his body duly matched with his position. Yes, the lips that covered the protruding sets of teeth looked a little odd but that didn't qualify him for a monkey.

The winter evening of London shouldn't be trifled with. With the deepening of night, cold increases. However, inside home it felt very cozy; the more time one spent in the drawing room the better. Pareshnath didn't feel like leaving the place. He could visualize his friends and probationers in the office eyeing him with jealousy. It was as if they all knew who the goddess of warmth was. Shashwatee, the daughter of his boss, was young and beautiful. Abani Dasa, Pareshnath's colleague, taking a dig at the good fortune of the latter once said, "It's true that I took birth as a 'Dasa' (referring to his title) but I couldn't become a faithful '*dasa*' or servant otherwise, I would have been sent to London in your place. In that case, I would have met her.

"Oh, how vicious their thoughts are! Am not I different from them? They have forgotten that I am magnanimous. How can I forget the lessons in morals and manners imparted by my father and grandfather? I don't appreciate the beauty that is divested of manners." He felt so uncomfortable inside that he decided to escape to the cold outside. Pareshnath decided that he shouldn't make any further delays in carrying out the orders of his boss. The lady must have understood by now that he wasn't the type of person to put up with her impudence. So, as if in a great hurry, he asked, "What should I inform your father when I meet him? Should I tell him that you are well and you have absolutely no problems? By the way, if you have any letters to send him you can hand over those to me by Tuesday…"

Shashwatee wasn't ready to reply. She was examining the family photograph that Pareshnath had handed her. It was a family photo that his boss had asked him to hand over to her. At the sight of that photo, she had made such a repulsive remark.

Surprising! Doesn't the lady have an idea of good conduct? I asked her so many questions but why she has turned a deaf ear to those? Does she think I'm her father's servant? Pareshnath's anger intensified. His anger didn't show any sign of dissipating because he marked that she not only was ill-mannered but also was shameless. She was so much engrossed in the photo that she didn't mark when her saree had slipped, exposing her bosom. She had bent down to such an extent on the centre-table that her cleavage was clearly visible. Pareshnath grew scared to think that if Shashwatee bent down further, it would become impossible for him to avoid her.

What did she examine so much? Was it her father's monkeyish face or mother's charming face? Perhaps she wanted to find out if she had taken after her mother and how much she resembled her. No matter how much she searched she would never find an iota of their charm and decency in her. How could she? How could a daughter speak so ill of her father?

Pareshnath's fears were proved unfounded. She soon straightened and covered her bosom with folds of her saree. She answered, "Yes, please tell him that I'm well. There is absolutely nothing to worry. Can you please hand over this letter to my mother? Thanks."

Shashwatee stood up as if intending to say, "The interview is over. You may go now". Pareshnath understood that he had to bid goodbye to the coziness of the drawing room and step into the cold streets. He had already been offered a cup of tea. His questions had already been answered. A courtesy-exhibiting smile had accompanied the answers although it didn't matter whether they were to his satisfaction or not. What else was expected? Why should he bother so much about the remark that she had made about her father? "It's my wish that matters. I have every right to say whatever I wish. What doubts do you harbor about my personality when I'm standing right in front of you?"

Pareshnath was able to perceive the personality she was proud of—her length, breadth and complexion. "Is it what you call your personality? Is it what you are proud of? The figure of yours! That you are five feet six or seven inches tall...that you have a certain breadth... that you have a certain girth...I'm not interested in these physicalities. Certain personalities command respect. Heads automatically bow down before them in respect. The words floating out of their lips, whether sweet or sour, appear to have a veneer of truth. Their smiles, even when razor sharp, don't cause any pain. Their looks, even when reflect the seething anger within, don't create any aversion. Irrespective of the situation, one seeks refuge in such personalities. Your personality doesn't incite any such feelings. I'm not the kind of person who gives in only to one's femininity. Besides, the lady who can utter such..."

Pareshnath found himself hesitant to leave the place

instantaneously. He had some duty towards his boss. No matter how reproving the lady sounded, he must make a careful scrutiny of the surroundings. This would give him enough idea as to how she was. She was living as a paying guest in an old lady's house in Windsor Crescent in North London. A respectable locality, no doubt. Many wealthy Gujaratis, who had fled from Kenya, lived here. Most of them owned palatial buildings and cinemas. Residence in such a locality was certainly going to have some influence of Indian Culture. In one corner, he found a record player. A record pulled out of its cover lay nearby (its music was boisterous). A block of cheese, half-used, lay there (Food meant sandwich and cooking was considered out of fashion). Some art calendars (art, my foot! Only photos of sturdy bachelors) adorned the wall. What's this book lying on the table? It's titled *Deviant Behaviour* (Bah! The most suitable one for a lady like you). Why should one who has come to attain a Post Graduate degree in Economics read such a book?"

So many things remain to be noted but they hardly matter. Your character can be well-portrayed from what I heard and saw here. Everything can't be divulged to your father, though. During the last twenty-five years, I've come across many human beings but none like you. You are so vastly different.

Pareshnath could have taken the Tube-Rail from the nearby station but he decided to walk so that he could confront the cold breeze that sent shivers down the spine. He hated to be vanquished. What did Shashwatee think of herself? She was a mere tall, charming lady. Very soon, she'll get married and transform herself into a tall woman, bear children and have a family of her own. What more was expected from her? If by chance, she decided to go for a job and remain unmarried, would there be a change of fortune? Hunger of the body would invite untimely old age. Her youthful charm would wither; dark circles would appear below her eyes; her wrinkled skin would hang loose. Her world would be surrounded by grief, regrets, indignation and tears that she had refused to shed earlier.

No matter how much he tried to denigrate Shashwatee, she would penetrate into his world of imagination every time and stand before his eyes with a display of her personality.

The frequent displays of her personality became so intolerable that Pareshnath thought of the ladies working in shops in Soho square and compared her with them. "Oh! It seems you wish to be like them." If one follows the invitation of blinking lights announcing 'Sex. Sex. Sex' and enters inside, one discovers innumerable photographs of tall, nude, glistening bodies of beautiful girls. Tomorrow is Sunday. Will those shops be closed for the day? Won't there be secret doors to go inside? I'll surely buy a book and show my friends in India as to how the society has denigrated. Your personality is no different from that of these ladies. You are made of the same stuff. Everything about you is obscene."

Damn her! Once I return to India, I'll teach her a lesson.

A few years had passed before Paresh met Shashwatee in Delhi. In the meantime, he had collected as much information about her as he could. A friend of the neighbor's son of the Boss had provided much clue. Some information came through the Compounder of his Boss' family doctor. Even a gentleman, who belonged to his boss's native place, provided vital information. Even the Boss himself spoke about her behavior at times. An analysis of their opinions helped him draw one conclusion. The remark that Shashwatee made about her father at London wasn't an act of 'ordinary impudence' or 'extraordinary childishness'. She hated her father despite being his only daughter. The Boss had two sons but there was nothing to prove that they loved him. She was the most insolent to him. She not only made fun of his abnormal face but his education, his wisdom, and even his blood-pressure. She was once heard saying that her father read whatever renowned writers wrote on the dust-jackets of their books but while speaking to outsiders, he would behave as if he had read the book thoroughly. Besides, she believed that the illness he talked about was fake; it was only a way to flee from home and spend some time in the club. This was a plea for avoiding mother. Indirectly, she would convey that her mother was not only beautiful but also unfortunate. On the other hand, her father was not only monkey-faced but also no less than an animal. However, it was never explicit why her mother felt cheated or how she was impacted by his animality. Pareshnath also had the information that she was a voracious reader; she didn't have any intimate friends or even, boy-friends. Among the young men she was more recognized as an 'untouchable'. Pareshnath congratulated himself as whatever ideas he had gathered about Shashwatee at the first meeting were more or less confirmed.

Pareshnath held dear the information that he got from his Boss one day. It was, for him, an invaluable treasure. Even though he couldn't understand the underlying meaning he was confident that, one day or the other, it would throw light on some hidden secret. His Boss was sitting in a relaxed posture and smoking a cigar. He was lost in the void of the closing hour of the office. The moment Paresh removed the curtain and peeped into the chamber, he called him in and welcomed him with a prolonged smile. He spoke in detail about the invention of the astrologer; how stars didn't die, how the black-hole still existed after the death of the star; how it was believed that the color of the soul was black and many other novel and startling ideas. He would smoke his pipe and flash a smile at times. Pareshnath was bowled over by his scholarship and thought that such a great genius was wasting his talent in a government office. His Boss said, "Both my sons were interested in make-believe games of the solar system. They would play with colored balls. I would inspire them with these games. But Shashwatee wasn't interested in those. She preferred dolls instead — not the dolls that usually girls of her age play with but animal-dolls. Donkeys, horses, sheep, pigs, dogs and foxes were her playmates. She wished to have neither human-dolls nor vehicles. She only appreciated animal-dolls." He said this, nodded his head and burst out into a laugh, perhaps at the memory of those days. What a crazy girl she was to play with animal-dolls!

Pareshnath wished to ask if a monkey was ever included in the paraphernalia but he would desist from asking this.

Many a time, Pareshnath had thought of bringing a monkey into the gamut of their discussion. He thought of telling him how his dear daughter valued him. But his Boss was well aware of her feelings. Besides, at the mention of such things, a father's resplendent face was sure to wither, for a moment though. "No, I can never cause him pain." It may so happen that she had a nightmare in her childhood concerning her father. Perhaps she bore witness to some physical torture that remained etched in her sub-conscious. Perhaps her father had ignored her mother and hobnobbed with another woman. His confusion deepened as he had known his Boss to be an intelligent and kind-hearted person. It's difficult to fathom he could have indulged in something so disgusting. Pareshnath thought neither the self-conceited daughter nor her mother could despoil his image. He himself had unnecessarily been dragged into a controversy between a man and a woman. He decided to follow his dharma—he would never desert his Boss.

With the passage of time, Pareshnath rose higher in the professional-ladder. He had to leave Delhi on transfer and go to Kolkatta, and from Kolkatta to Patna. He served in various positions under the central government. No matter where he was posted, all information concerning his Boss would inevitably reach him. Once he heard that his Boss was going to become the secretary of the department. Later he learnt that he could not become so. He was famed for being fearless and outspoken. Which minister would like to face unnecessary trouble! On another occasion, he heard about the untimely death of his Boss' wife. He wrote a letter expressing his deepest condolences. However, he restrained himself from asking him to have courage and forbearance. He knew his Boss was like a banyan tree. No... no...not a banyan tree but a pine tree. No misfortune could bend him down.

Pareshnath had never thought that the situation would change so much by the time he next met Shashwatee; it'd be considered savage even to smile, forget about taking up a conversation. He had come to Delhi to meet his former Boss, who had by then retired. Unfortunately, before he could meet him, he had left this world for his heavenly abode. He consoled himself saying that such a sudden death was usual with patients with high blood pressure. He thought, "By the time I reach there, many other officers would have assembled. It wouldn't be possible to pay last respects to him alone. Who would understand that I wasn't an ordinary officer but a close confidant? It would also not be possible to mark the reaction of Shashwatee."

Pareshnath wasn't much surprised when he heard from someone that Shashwatee had returned to India. She worked in Jawaharlal Nehru University and lived in a rented accommodation. However, he was certain that she would be there by his deathbed. She was after all his flesh and blood.

Pareshnath felt delighted within, when he discovered Shashwatee amidst the mourners. Didn't I tell you? She was, after all, a human being, a woman! Later, he felt ashamed of himself thinking that she would have marked his cheery face and misunderstood him. There's no way he could dispel her misunderstanding. He daren't go close to her any longer; he only eyed her secretly from a distance. Her face appeared swollen, true but do you think it hadn't even an iota of grief? Does one's face wither or wilt in a day? Of course, streams of tear were expected on such occasions, but amidst such a large crowd, wasn't it absurd? Rather, her restraint was praiseworthy.

Pareshnath was desperately trying to prove that the childish-rebel of London had grown up and undergone transformation. There's no reason why she should be subject to so much censure, then.

Pareshnath went in and out with the visitors, stood with his hands crossed near the dead body, reminisced about the past, and marked the grief-stricken face of Shashwatee as much as possible. Then something interesting happened. A VIP visited the dead body to pay his last respects. The gentleman looked at the face of the dead body and remarked, "How charming it looks! As fresh as a rose!" Pareshnath immediately turned his face towards Shashwatee to mark her reaction. She concentrated her gaze on her father's face and mumbled a 'yes'. Pareshnath thought perhaps his blood pressure had spread much blood through the body and consequently, the dead body looked fresh. However, he couldn't disregard Shashwatee's love and compassion for her father. "How peacefully lies my monkey-faced father! How charming his face appears today!"

Much water had flowed down the river since then. Pareshnath had got married and become a father. He had subordinates who addressed him as 'Sir'. He occupied various positions not only in India but also abroad, and travelled around the world. He has acquired enough experience about the honesty as well as malevolence of men. The strange behavior of a person doesn't startle him up anymore. Almost everyone possesses the same characteristics. Only relationship matters. What counts is whether one is my steno or my boss; whether he's a leader or a servant; whether she's Rukmini or Radha?" Accordingly, one has to change appearances. Can one distinguish between the noble and the supercilious; between the magnanimous and the ordinary under such circumstances?

These days, Pareshnath is rarely reminded of Shashwatee, or the special way his ex-Boss uttered each syllable. He considers them interesting. But much before the feeling of delight seeps in, he relieves the memories and once again remains absorbed in worldly affairs.

Despite the advancing age and growing concerns, Pareshnath finds it impossible to erase Shashwatee completely from his memory. He is reminded of the scene of the death-bed of his Boss. "I have already forgiven you. Why are you putting me in further trouble?" Finally, he thinks that she must have got married in the meantime and borne many children. The thought of a married Shashwatee makes him feel a bit relaxed but the very next moment he fosters the desire that she should remain a 'character' in his dreams without deserting him completely and leaving him forlorn.

After Pareshnath was transferred to Guwahati, many things remained to be done on a priority basis including submission of transfer TA bill, arrangement of furniture, besides a visit to the famous Kamakshya temple. Vibha frequently asked him not to wait for her but to have a *darshan* of the deity. At first Pareshnath thought it wasn't imperative on his part to visit the temple alone because goddess Kamakshya liked couples as she was the deity of deep love and desire. She was shaped as a 'yoni,' a female genital. However, he didn't wait for Vibha. Perhaps he was in a hurry to pay a visit to the charming goddess.

One Bhadrab morning, Pareshnath decided to have a *darshan* of the deity. The temple was situated atop a mountain. One has to go to a deep, dark place to have her *darshan*. He felt exasperated as he was shoved and elbowed while moving through a dark and narrow tunnel. A couple of devotees were found discussing, "She is the only goddess who doesn't have a visage or a figure. She's called the goddess of illusions". He nodded his head to indicate he had understood the implications of their statement.

When he, after waiting in the serpentine queue for

his turn, reached the destination and saw water in the inner chamber, he felt relaxed. However, the people standing in front of him were showing no signs of moving ahead. When he looked ahead to see what really had happened, he found a couple at the front, not willing to move eve an inch. They were in no mood to sip a little water and move, as the custom is; they religiously followed whatever the Panda asked them to do. They kneeled down, touched the holy water, sprinkled a little on each other, chanted mantras and kneeled down again. To hell with them! Were they the first ones to get married? Was goddess Kamakshya going to listen to their prayers only?

Finally, they got up to go. Pareshnath stepped forward. There was no need of kneeling down. He had to touch the water with the tip of his fingers and sprinkle a little on him. But before he had accomplished the task, his eyes fell on the face of the woman. Did he know her? A quick examination revealed it was Shashwatee. How impossible! Absurd!

It was as absurd, inconceivable and unbelievable as it could be. It was as absurd as a fairytale turning real; a mouse nibbling at the moon; and the sun shooting one arrow after another. Shashwatee stood and smiled profusely. He recognized Pareshnath. He returned her greetings but not a single word emerged from his lips. She indicated him to come out so that they could talk.

What was there to be surprised? I had already assigned her the role of a married woman; I had wished her to be the part of a ladies' community. It's true that she had got married at an advanced age of forty but wasn't that a marriageable age? Now she was bending before the goddess seeking her blessings and praying for the long life of her husband. Her orange-colored silk saree had got stained at the knees but that was hardly a worry. A small dry clean job!

Why wouldn't she smile her heart out? Was she expected to move about with a face weighed down in grief? It's true that she has become double-chinned and has layers of fat with sweat emanating from those but that doesn't disqualify her from being a woman. Only there was some problem somewhere. What was it? Was it some disorder or mishap or psychology or Freud or something else?

Shashwati was waiting for him outside. How modest and polite she had become! The moment she saw him, she introduced her husband to him, "Meet my husband..."

'Ugly' was too meager a word to describe that man. Pareshnath wished to smile...a hearty smile. Forget about a monkey, he looked worse than a gorilla or a chimpanzee. The lady who didn't hesitate to take a dig at her father by calling him a monkey, had married such a person...how ridiculous!

Shashwati continued, "This is Narottam Barua." She didn't divulge much on his profession. She got married two months ago; left the university job at Delhi. She'll work here, stay here...this place has a strong resemblance with Ireland, doesn't it? Pareshnath wanted to say that he had never been to Ireland and so, he couldn't perhaps have an opinion. Newly married as she was, the place must look like garden of heaven to her. But he remained silent. He examined Narottam from head to feet and found that he was a silly, half-witted fool. His nose was flat; his look didn't reflect a trace of wisdom. It seemed she had married him only because he was foolish. Perhaps she wanted to have absolute control over him. She wanted an animal-doll to play with. For her, men should be half-wits so that she could use them as puppets. Perhaps, that's why she was jealous of his quick-witted father and made fun of him by calling him a monkey. Only after his death that she showed any compassion. Pareshnath brightened up as if he had got answers to an incomprehensible question.

What had you remarked about her? Arrogant and self-conceited! Worthy of being despised and detested for a life time! Why did the fountain of hate dry up then?

Yes, I'm really extremely thrilled. If people can be identical in nature, why can't there be someone who is dissimilar? For the last twenty years, she hasn't changed. She is different from others; unchanging too. She derives pleasure when she lords over men. Nowhere have I remarked that she is commonplace. I'll treat her both as a demon and as a deity. I'll censure her whenever I wish. I'll treat her as a deity whenever I wish, too and submit myself at her feet. Like a goddess she is intelligent, beautiful, bold, animated and luminous...

You must pay us a visit. Both of them—the woman and the fool, entreated with folded hands, flashing smiles. Pareshnath nodded frequently, without restraint.

I'll certainly visit them. Of course, I won't be able to defeat her. Before I meet them, I'll transform Vibha into Shashwatee. Vibha must have a layer of fat all over her body so that she looks forty.

❑

(Original Odia: *Shashwatee*)

The Sulking Mounabati

Achyutananda Pati

The intensely sulking princess of Ranga Island lay in the bedstead with her face buried in the bed-linen. She had already made up her mind—she would rather snuff herself out than marry someone and set up a family in a land where no one respected light. In other words, she would rather die than barter her heart with some worthless young man. Should she gobble up some cheap food like spinach or pith of plantain or spinage or *ambade* in the absence of food meet for a princess? She had veiled herself with a firmness of purpose—a firmness that is conspicuous in noble blood. She had grown up in a palace surrounded by its tall and iron-strong compound walls. In the sanctum sanctorum of the palace temple that looked resplendent with its white marbles, she had worshipped the crystal phallus image and offered it golden champak flowers for twenty years. During these twenty years, she had never ever got an opportunity to look beyond the compound wall, even for a second, to have a glimpse of the world beyond. She had heard from her attendants and maid-servants that in that world, evil permeated everywhere and venomous serpents spewed out their venoms all around. There was no dearth of instances of falsehood, thievery, spitefulness and conflicts. If she exposed herself to these, drops of foul-smelling mud would surely stick to her turmeric-colored body. She assumed that there was greater pride in getting extinguished on her own in the confines of the palace than to be blown down by the smoke, the dew or the stormy winds of the outer world. At first, she was scared of venturing outside. Gradually, her connections with the outer world were completely snapped. With the pickaxe of ethics, she dug up her holy-pond and remained completely submerged in its waters.

The king was greatly perturbed by the adamant princess and her manners. A mature maiden as she had grown up to, it was expected that she would marry someone and take charge of the hearth at the in-laws' place. It is natural on the part of a woman to grow up at her parents' place before proceeding to the in-laws' place on attaining youth. The feelings that this maiden harbored in her heart were against the norms of the world. She was bent upon not even opening her heart to young men of this world, forget about accepting one as husband. The queen tried her best to coax and cajole her daughter by reminding her frequently, 'A woman's life attains fullness in her journey from her parents' place to her in-laws' place'. Despite her sincere efforts, the princess insisted on marrying none.

The king consulted his senior ministers. Finally, he issued a proclamation. He got it announced through beating of drums that anyone who appeased the wrath of his daughter will be given her in marriage. Just as the flood waters cross one boundary ridge after another and inundate the fields, the news spread from one country to another. There was a hue and cry everywhere: "The one who appeases the wrath of Mounabati's indignation will be fortunate to hold her in her lap!"

Many young princes, donning gorgeous clothes, came from different states and gathered at the entrance to Ranga Island. When their turn came, they were ushered into the princess' chamber, where they presented erudite lectures on the *Gita*, the *Mahabharat*, the scriptures and the *Puranas*. They had secretly collected the information that the princess was highly educated; she would never budge until she was thoroughly convinced with their arguments. Prior to visiting the Ranga Island, they had invited learned scholars to their palaces, honored them with presents of silk clothes and expensive ear-rings, and learnt from them the intricacies of these texts. The princess watched the display of intellect amusedly. At the sight of venomous serpents, snake-charmers chant mantras to the accompaniment of a musical instrument made of gourd, in order to charm them. Similarly, at the sight of her repugnant serpent eyes they sang exalted lines from the scriptures. If their method proved effectual, they thought, she would surrender at their feet just as the charmed snake enters the snake-charmer's casket. Nights after nights passed but a disconcerted Mounabati remained disconsolate as ever. The princess, with the touchstone of her penetrating eyes, could peep within everyone and see the huge vacuum that pervaded within. They had adorned themselves with the gorgeous yellow silk clothing of fake knowledge, which they claimed to have acquired from the fat books. However, inside they possessed even little knowledge of the basics. Putting a veil on their ignorant minds they feigned wise ascetics. The princess hardly opened her lips to convey her opinion of them. Consequently, the avaricious princess would return, carrying the bare caskets of their knowledge. The handlebar moustaches with their upwardly curved extremities, which they proudly displayed on their approach, hung loose like *siuli* flowers, ready to be shed, by the end of the night. The princes scurried off, like soldiers vanquished in the battle-field, with heads bent down.

A young gardener working in the royal garden had been secretly keeping an eye on the activities of the princess. With his knowledge of astrology, he calculated that a phony ideal had nested in the princess' mind. Just as white milk, after being boiled for a long time, turns yellowish and has a thin layer of cream on the surface, similarly the fake ideal had coagulated in her mind. Finally, the young gardener placed his candidature and made a request that he be given an opportunity to amuse the sulking princess. The king allowed him to enter the inner chambers of the princess and hold discussions with her. The young gardener explained details of his plans to four of his friends and took them with him as his assistants. Without the knowledge of the princess, he hid them near the four legs of the bedstead. This he could do by bribing the maid-servant most intimate to the princess. He had trained them beforehand to answer whatever questions he aimed at them.

The final moments arrived; night got ready to descend upon the earth. 'The death of one ensures life to another.' This is the rule that has governed human civilization since time immemorial. In the race-course of this civilization, the one who commits the greatest number of murders lives with the greatest pride and is said to have ennobled his life.

It was the first quarter of the night when the young gardener started his presentation.

Story of the First Quarter

Once there lived a mighty king. There was no dearth of riches, manpower, concubines, maid-servants or cattle. Goddess Lakshmi showered on him her choicest blessings. Kings are usually unrelenting. How can this king of ours be without this quality? If he presumed something to be correct, others were bound to accept it as correct. Even he compelled another person, by twisting his ears, to believe that it was correct. He had assumed that the poor people of his kingdom were made for slogging. They were no better than donkeys and pigs. To set them to hard work and drive them to a state of helplessness were his only aims. He would capture such poor helpless people and force them to slog.

Once, the king came across such a poor person and ordered him to work in the royal garden. From very early in the morning till evening, he worked there. He would prepare the soil, plant seeds and grow fruits and vegetables. After the work was over, he would go to the king's presence and beg, with folded hands, to be paid his wages. After the court proceedings were over, the following words would emerge from the mouth of the esteemed king, "Come tomorrow, it'll be taken care of". When the mother vulture returns to her nest after a search for prey, her babies usually clamor, "Give us the food you have brought, Mother". They hardly understand that their mother's search for prey has gone in vain. She comforts and consoles her hungry children saying, "So and so is going to die tomorrow. Eat to your fill then. Please keep a check on your hunger for today." That poor man would console his children everyday saying he would cook rice, dal and *kheer* as well as bake cakes for them once he received his wages from the king. He had to dispose of anything worthwhile that the family possessed and arrange food for his children. Since most of the time the food was insufficient even for the children, the couple would sleep in empty stomachs. The king's 'tomorrow' never turned 'today'. He received no wages from the palace and lived in deep distress. With no food in his tommy, he had not much strength left in him. Consequently, he couldn't please the master with his work anymore. Forget about relief, he was flogged by his master.

Once, the children had nothing to eat throughout the day. In hunger, they had all wilted. As a father how he could tolerate this! With no other solution at sight, he stole a gourd from the royal garden. The informers passed the information to the king within no time. Before the boiled gourd slices could land on his children's plates, he was arrested by the soldiers and presented before the king. He accepted his guilt without any qualms. The educated officials working in the king's court quoted volubly, while belching in full stomach, from the ancient texts of Manu and Parashar.

It was ordered that his right hand be chopped off.

The young gardener finished his story and asked the first leg of the bedstead, "Tell me, O honored leg of Mounabati's bedstead, whether the punishment meted out to the poor man was just or unjust?"

The friend hiding near the first leg shot back, "In my opinion, the punishment is just as thieving is a sin".

Mounabati staggered a little. "No, this is injustice," she thought. Her lips trembled but she didn't open her mouth to express her opinion. She composed herself.

The young gardener didn't lose hope. He realized that the princess' fountain of love had gone dry. Stones blocked its path. He raised his crowbar to remove the stone and let it flow unhindered. He started another story in the second quarter of the night.

Story of the Second Quarter

There was another king. He was extremely upright and noble. He had given ample freedom to his officials and soldiers to indulge in tyranny. They rode horses and roamed around villages and collected multifarious taxes from people. Besides land-tax, they forcibly collected betel-tax, *biri*-tax, intoxicants tax, smile-tax and many such taxes as per their whims and fancies. The king was always busy in wine, women and his business ventures. His concern about the affairs of the state was limited to imposing new taxes only.

The officials displayed tremendous alacrity in abducting maidens and women from the streets and presenting them to the king for his nightly-pleasures. The villagers would lock their doors and flee the moment they heard that the king's men were heading towards their village. So deep was the fear among the people that some of them would faint when the soldiers approached.

The worries of the parents would increase manifold if a beautiful girl was born into the family. They would disfigure the girl's face by drawing tattoos or by branding it with burning hot pebbles. The girl's father, brother or guardian was supposed to accompany the girl when she was carried to the *Rang Mahal*. They had to wait anxiously, in an empty stomach, outside the entrance while inside their child was devoured by the king and the ministers throughout the night. Towards dawn, the unconscious or dying maiden would be thrown up to the waiting relative.

One day, an official of the king's court arrived with a summon requiring the daughter of a destitute widow to report at the *Rang Mahal*. The widow worked in people's houses and with her meager income both of them would somehow manage themselves. They would provide a helping hand to the villagers in their weal and woe and voluntarily undertake many tasks. Naturally, the villagers were full of compassion for them.

When the king's official insisted on taking the maiden with him, both mother and daughter cried horrendously and locked themselves in an embrace. The official's heart refused to melt.

The official started tugging the girl towards him. The village young men, on finding the honor of the village at stake, fought with him and drove him away. Defeated and flustered, he ran back to the palace. On the other hand, the villagers grew terror-stricken. Some people, living close to the palace, reported that the soldiers were getting ready with arms and ammunitions to destroy the village. The villagers fled and hid behind bushes. However, the maiden's mother didn't wish to leave the village even though she knew what consequences she would suffer for her defiance.

Just as an oil-lamp burns brighter before dousing, similarly she was determined to teach the king a lesson before being punished with death. The king had already passed an order to the guards to present the maiden before him, alive. He wouldn't mind if some villagers had to murdered in the process. The guards got off their horses, searched for the maiden here and there and finally got hold of her mother. Lashes after lashes fell on the old lady's back. She was repeatedly questioned about the whereabouts of the villagers and her daughter but every time she came out with the only answer that she had no knowledge of them. Tying the lady's blood-streaming body to the horse, the guards galloped to the palace. When they reached the Lion's Gate of the palace, they found only one leg; the body was missing.

After the story was over, the young gardener looked at the princess briefly and asked, "O honored leg of the princess' bedstead, tell me if the right kind of punishment has been meted out to the lady."

The young man's friend hiding under the bed answered, "It's a sin to tell a lie. In my opinion, the right kind of punishment has been meted out to the lady."

The princess raised her face, wrinkly and crumpled, for a while and then buried it in the pillows. In front of her eyes galloped the king's tall horses. Streams of blood and lumps of flesh lay scattered along the way to the palace. In her heart of hearts, she realized that injustice had been perpetrated. Nevertheless, she remained mum.

Water takes the color of the bottle into which it is poured. Similarly, viewed through the fractured ethics of the princess, the pious souls of persons appeared distorted. The young gardener was confident that he would uncork the bottle and lead the princess' heart from darkness to humanity.

He started narrating his third story in the third quarter of the night.

Story of the Third Quarter

This is also the story of a strange king. People of his kingdom shuddered when his name was pronounced. He was one who derived a great delight from the troubles of others. His court was a collection of blockheads. It was a place where great conspiracies were hatched and undeserving idiots were handsomely rewarded.

This king of ours was absolutely fascinated by the game of dice. He had employed four people whose only task was to remain in a state of absolute readiness with the dice and the dice board. Whenever the king desired, he would arrive and take his place at the dice board. One of the above four players would hand over the dice to the king and move away. The king was such an accomplished player that he never earned a negative point. Every time he threw, he scored enough to dismantle the counters of the opposition. The other three players had no qualms in accepting that the king had in fact scored the required points. The king handsomely rewarded those who moved his counters to the required box which would help him to score over others.

A poor Brahmin happened to be the king's friend. Both of them, as children, were students of the same school. Once, the king was reminded of his friend. He sent an orderly to fetch him. When the Brahmin appeared in the king's palace, he was asked to participate in a game of dice. Although he was utterly confused about the real intention of the king, he decided to participate in the game.

It so happened that the pet dog of the Brahmin reached the palace after him. It met the king's dog on the way. It's natural that when two unknown dogs meet each other, they indulge in a fight. Initially the king's dog and the Brahmin's dog tried to scare each other away but then they indulged in a full-fledged fight. The Brahmin's dog sprang upon the king's dog and bit it fiercely a few times. The king's dog fled from the spot with its tail between the legs. News of what the Brahmin's dog had done spread far and wide within minutes. People came to know how the dog that lived on the froth of boiled rice overpowered the flesh-eating dog of the king. How could the unscrupulous ministers let go such an opportunity to harm someone? They whispered into the King's ears the proud and insolent way the Brahmin had acted; they also presented a list of remedial measures the King could take to restore his honor.

The King, in an attempt to teach the impudent Brahmin a lesson, intensified his attacks on him. The poor man's hut was set on fire that night. Ripe crops were cut and carried away from his fields. The milch cow that sustained him was confiscated by the state. Still then the King was not satisfied. Despite the repressive measured adopted by the king, the Brahmin didn't reach the palace or apologize for the harm he had done. The King, incited by the ministers, became extremely brutal. He entrusted the task of finishing off the only son of the Brahmin to some assassins. At the dead of night these criminals broke open the door of the Brahmin's hut, entered inside and attempted to abduct his infant son. The Brahmin's wife, on getting a whiff of their mission, cried horrendously and fell at their feet requesting them to let go their only son. Since, she continued to prove a hindrance in the accomplishment of their task, they finished her off first. The Brahmin wasn't at home then. He suddenly arrived and finding the dead body of his wife on the ground, attacked the intruders and killed one of them. He was charged with treason and homicide. He was captured and dragged to the King's court. There was enough evidence against him. So, he was punished with death by hanging.

After narrating this tale, the young gardener asked

the third leg of Mounabati's bedstead what he felt about the dispensation of justice to the Brahmin. The reply that came was, "Violence is a sin and since the Brahmin had perpetrated it, his punishment was just."

Mounabati, at this point, was found moaning. She beat her head on the pillow and sobbed.

The night had entered its fourth phase. The nails on the princess' heart were gradually loosening. The young gardener had an inkling of his impending success. Feeling delighted at the prospect of this probable success he searched his quiver for the last arrow. He started narrating the story of the fourth quarter.

Story of the Fourth Quarter

This is the secret story of another kingdom. The king had a large number of concubines besides his queens. The concubines always spread the fragrance of *Phalguna* in the inner chambers of the palace with bouquets of their beauty. The king sucked the drips of their fragrance just as the bees suck honey from flowers. He however didn't have the ability to suck all the honey from all the flowers of his garden. Despite this, the king could never do away with his fascination for flowers. He never wished to lose possession of a single flower. The bee's special fascination for certain flowers enraged others and filled them with jealousy. However, they couldn't muster courage to rise up against the bee.

Among the king's concubines there was one who was adorned with a youthful vigor and passionate desire. The problem with her was that the king hardly ever had the time to visit her bower. The king ensured that all queens and concubines enjoyed the best of facilities. There was no dearth of food, drinks, clothes or even, servants. There was everything to boast of but very little companionship of the king.

An innocent young man was employed to run errands for one of them. His young muscular physique and youthful vigor often filled the concubine's mind with flirtatious thoughts. The insatiate concubine would often hunger for physical proximity with him. The young man, on the other hand, was not only poor but also unmindful of her desires. No matter how much she tried to entrap him, he remained at a safe distance. The young man lived with his young wife. The couple somehow managed themselves with the meager salary that he received from the palace. His wife had to work in peoples' houses to augment their income. Amidst all kinds of paucities, they had but one thing in plenty-- it's 'love' that sustained their relationship. They bore in their hearts love, affection and concern for each other. Just as a young bird couple constructs its nest on some thorny plants, unmindful of its pricking thorns, similarly this young couple lived a life of zest, unwearied about the problems of life.

The concubine left no stones unturned to entice the young man. She would intentionally drop her clothes off at times, exposing her tender flesh. She would bump into him at other times. She would tempt him with her dark inviting eyes. However, the young man would remain nonchalant all the time.

It so happened once that the young man's wife suddenly fell ill. Her condition worsened day by day. The Ayurveda practitioner consulted his books and pronounced that she had contracted typhoid. He handed him over a list of expensive medicines needed for her cure. Where would he get so much money to buy such medicines? The next day, he conveyed his difficulties to the concubine. Taking advantage of his troubles, she made him her victim. The young man was compelled to do as he was asked to, thinking of his ailing wife. The youngest queen's maid-servant, on entering the concubine's chamber one day, found them in a compromising position.

At the sight of the queen's maid, the concubine shouted, "Please save me…save me." The servants and attendants working in the palace gathered there. They dragged the young man by his hair and presented him before the king. The concubine complained to the king that the young man had been trying to outrage her modesty. The king flew into a rage and ordered that both his eyes be gouged out.

After the tale was told, the young gardener asked the wise fourth leg of the bedstead to tell him if justice had been done with the young man.

The fourth friend hiding under the bed solemnly answered, "It's a grave sin to molest another's wife. The young man deserved more punishment for the crime he had committed."

Mounabati suddenly got off the bedstead. She blurted out, "No…no…this is all absurd, unreasonable and unjust."

The young gardener flashed a smile and said, "Dear Princess, according to the condition laid down by your father, you become mine from this instant. As my companion, I request you to listen to me carefully."

The tales that I narrated are related to your father. He has provided you golden champak flowers to worship the crystal phallus image of lord Shiva. They have covered your eyes with the false veil of distorted notions and ethics. They have never allowed you to venture into the real world on the pretext that it is muddy and miry. On the other hand, they have lived in the mud and enjoyed their lives.

You have seen the fake lotus-filled-tank covered with holy leaves at the top but with seven fathom deep mud at the bottom. The sight of the golden grafted petals has affected your dream. Consequently, you have always loathed the innocent grass blossoms as if they were infested with pests. Your exposure to horses, elephants and swings in the sham-world has created an aversion and abhorrence for the world. You have never known what sin actually is. The sin-infested people have presented you a fake portrait of sin.

Let's get away from this world and wander around in the other world. You might encounter resistance from some who have thrived on sucking blood of the innocent citizens. In the other world, I can show you many buildings that resemble the palace within the strong protective boundary wall, where human beings are sacrificed in the sacrificial pit.

Only when the rains wash off the vague tints with which you have colored your heart, you can have an earnest appreciation of someone else's heart.

Dawn had already broken. The princess had crossed the Lion's gate of the palace and was proceeding towards the world that lay beyond it, hand in hand with the young gardener.

The blood red hues of the morning sun lent them a fresh tint.

❏

(Original Odia: *Mounabatira Mana*)

The Final Offering at Vrindavan

Mahapatra Nilamani Sahu

The moment a banging sound was heard from the front gate, Raghu lifted his face from the *Rama Krishna Lilamrit* book that he was reading and turned his gaze in that direction. The intruder shut the gate carefully and headed towards the latter. Raghu felt a little irritated. Who this could be at this hour of the day! Almost every other day he had to treat someone or the other as a guest. Someone had paid him a visit last evening. He was seen off at the bus-stop only this morning, after breakfast. Oh, how disgusting! These people won't allow him a moment of peace. Such visits are common when a person lives in a town close to his birthplace. Almost everyone who visits the town on some work drops in at some odd hour. All of those who had some court-work or a patient in the hospital or had his son writing an examination or come to admit his son in a college, paid visits unfailingly. Even those who came to the town seeking for a bride or groom didn't forget to drop in at his address.

Even his children felt annoyed. They complained that they weren't able to concentrate in their studies; they could neither sleep nor take bath peacefully. They couldn't even visit the loo when they needed to. Forget about bedding and mosquito net, not a single visitor even brought their own towel or lungi for use at night. They would use his children's clothes, oil, soap and comb unhesitatingly. Once a visitor went away with his elder son's bicycle, without even bothering to inform him. That day, he had his practical examination at eight o' clock. Worst of all, his college was situated three kilometres away from home. Some visitors used the bathroom for hours together, brushing teeth, using the latrine, washing their clothes with soap and finally, washing themselves clean with soap. In the meantime, his middle-daughter would be getting late to catch her bus. Someone else would leave for the market with the son's slippers on, leaving his own worn out slippers behind. Consequently, he would be fuming.

Even they didn't allow Raghu a moment of peace. They would never leave him alone to read his *Rama Krishna Lilamrit* or listen to the *bhajans* on the radio. They would talk incessantly about the unending disputes in the village as well as the cases in the court. They would fill his mind with unnecessary bother.

It was Raghu's wife Subhadra who was the worst sufferer. She had to slog from six in the morning till midnight doing chores like cleaning the latrine, washing clothes, cleaning the house, cooking, serving the guests and dealing with the friends of the children. Drops of sweat would run down like a stream even in winter evenings. Her charming smile had disappeared long ago. Wrinkles of dread had adorned her forehead. Her eyes reflected her weariness and disgust. If a crow happened to sit on the compound wall and caw continuously while the children were having their breakfast, Subhadra would shout out angrily while shooing it away, "How many more guests do you want in the house?" True- she had spent her entire lifetime cooking for and serving to unwanted people. She had been married for the last twenty-six years; people from her father's family visited her only on three or four occasions. But, there was no let off from these uninvited people. How much one would toil in the kitchen? Besides, weren't the prices of commodities shooting up?

Poor Raghu! Subhadra believed he was just another Bholanath, the forgetful. He was always lost in his office work. He was hardly concerned about what was happening at home, who visited them, how the money was spent etc. When at home, he would be found relaxing on the couch and lost in the reading of some scripture. During the course of the reading, he would fall asleep. After returning from office, he would take snacks and a cup of tea. After that he would visit temples, *maths*, saints and sages. He hardly bothered about the affairs at home.

Subhadra, of course, couldn't be faulted with for all her allegations. Raghu's salary was hardly adequate to manage home smoothly throughout the month. There was nothing remarkable about their children. The two daughters, it seemed, wouldn't get suitable matches. There was hardly anything to boast of their appearances; besides, where would they get money to buy grooms? The loan that they had incurred on the marriage of their niece and for the obsequies-rituals of Raghu's parents had not been paid off fully. His retirement was only five years away. He could neither buy a house nor construct one for the family. The roof of the paternal home had been blown away in two cyclones. It had only two rooms. Subhadra, for some obscure reason, had lost her interest in the world. Her old limbs, growing tired on the slightest exhaustion, made her feel disillusioned. It seemed to her as if the world had lost its charm.

Before such disappointment could grip Raghu fully, he would burst into a smile and start telling the beads of a rosary that he had procured from *Badadanda* at Puri. He would be lost in chanting of the name of 'Ram'. So far as worldly affairs were concerned, he undoubtedly was a failure; in the field of divinity, he might score a little. Was it that easy? No. While telling the beads, Raghu would heave a sigh. During his lifetime, he could achieve nothing. He can never become successful even if he tried. How could one, who failed miserably in the worldly affairs, earn the grace of God so easily?

These demoralizing thoughts couldn't deter Raghu from telling the beads and chanting the name of Gods. He would continue with his reading of *Lilamrita* and *Bakyamrita* of Vivekananda or Ramakrishna. He would visit different *maths* and temples during the evening and join in the singing of *bhajans*. He knew pretty well that he wouldn't get any benefits. A failure in the worldly affairs, his pursuit of God would yield nothing. He was just an ordinary mortal. He was like the vast multitude of winged-ants that make a vain attempt to fly in the sky but relapse to the ground very soon.The thin, small wings lay on the ground like husk. Such a thought would bring an abrupt end to his worries, regrets and hopes. A strange sense of freedom and peace would envelop his mind. His worries would no longer weigh heavily on him.

Raghu marked that his contemporaries had far surpassed him in terms of worldly attainments. Even those who were born after him hadn't lagged behind others much. Those who had very little wealth to boast of a few years ago, were found enjoying their pleasures and comforts. There was no dearth of money in the hands of the villagers. Embankments had been constructed on both sides of Maluni river. Canals ran through agricultural fields. Agricultural production had risen. Markets had been set up. Trade and commerce had made the villagers wealthy. People earned enough money. Raghu had handed over his three-acre landed property to Babana Bhoi for share cropping. Initially, Babana would give him a part of the produce as his share. For the last two years, he had stopped even giving him a *gauni* of paddy. He claimed that the land legally belonged to him as he had been cultivating it for the last twelve years. Babana had three strong and sturdy sons. They had forcefully taken possession over the land. Raghu had lost hope that he would be able to release his land. Let them take whatever they wanted; he could neither engage himself in strife with them nor drag them to the court. He hadn't bought the land himself; his father had bought these. He was a renowned *pala* singer; he had procured these three acres of landed property with his own earnings. His father had passed away years ago.

But, was the land going to stay with Babana and his children forever? Who knew who would take possession of those in the future? Let them earn a living. The produce from the land would have been enjoyed by these winged-ants; they were being enjoyed by those winged-ants. Let them do what they wish; one day or the other, they would relapse to the ground. Raghu could never think ill of anyone. He could never judge who was wrong and who was right. He could never judge whether Babana was right in taking possession over the landed property that his father had earned. Consequently, he preferred to remain silent.

His inability to judge who was wrong and who was right compelled him to go mum. Completely mum! Not a single word emerged from his mouth. It was better to shut the eyes and chant the name of Ram or Shyam and tell the beads. It mattered little whether they were *rudraksh* beads or *tulsi* beads or red sandal wood beads. Scientists had discovered that telling of beads decreased blood pressure and the intensity of heart diseases. Raghu would smile a silent smile at this thought. If something decreases, let it decrease; if something increases, let it increase. Certain things will either increase or decrease until the ultimate end is reached.

The person who barged through the gate that day when Raghu was busy reading some anecdotes from the *Rama Krishna Lilamrit* was none other than Mayadhar Sarangi. Mayadhar belonged to his native village. Raghu took off his spectacles, wiped its glasses clean and looked again to confirm what he had seen. The moment he realized that it was indeed Mayadhar, his displeasure subsided, not fully though. Mayadhar was a childhood friend but addressed him as '*Bhaina*' as he was two years younger than Raghu. Like him, Mayadhar was a failure in life's battles. He had two daughters and two sons but none of them had any education worth the name. Mayadhar tried his hand at agriculture first, and subsequently, in a hotel business. In both these endeavors, he failed miserably. He was a noble human being—so noble that he ended up as a failure in life. He had to depend on laborers in his attempts at agriculture. Finally, when the calculations were made he found that he had paid more wages than what he earned. Later, he opened a hotel '*Bisudhh Hindu Bhojanalay*' in the market. He couldn't manage the business for three months even. Everyday many customers would arrive and dine in the restaurant but escape on various pretexts when the matter of payment came. Even school-going children and students of a nearby college didn't find it difficult to outwit him. He had to pull the shutters down as not a single penny reached his hands. He now managed his family by selling the wood apples and coconuts collected from his garden. His wife collected coconut-fibre from the locality and made ropes of those. They would prepare sacred threads and sell those for some money. Besides, they cultivated ginger in a part of their backyard and generated some money selling that. They even sold cow-dung cakes in the market. Raghu would feel irritated at Mayadhar's inability to manage his family. Like him, this Mayadhar Sarangi was another symbol of a failure in life's struggles.

Raghu harbored a sense of attachment for Mayadhar. Like him, he never spoke ill of anyone. He never borrowed things from others, nor did he make any demands on them. A tall, thin person he was, much like a betel-nut plant. Advancing age, poverty, failures in life had bowed him down. When not in conversation, he would chant the name of 'Krishna'. He was an incarnation of meekness!

Raghu got up from his chair and headed towards the gate to welcome him. Mayadhar wore a cotton Punjabi, torn at places and a not-so-clean cotton dhoti. When a child, he had joined the Congress and moved from village to village, spreading the message of Gandhiji. He would write songs on non-violence and patriotism and sing that himself. He would make thread using the spinning-wheel. He had dissociated himself from all types of campaigning. The only thing that kept him busy was chanting the name of God. He was more or less associated with *maths* and temples. He sang *bhajans* quite well. He also knew how to play the tabla, the harmonium, and the tambour. In short, both the childhood friends shared certain characteristics.

At the sight of the childhood friend, Raghu felt delighted. The feeling of disgust soon evaporated. About ten years ago, palsy had affected part of Mayadhar's face. Moved by the pathetic condition of his friend, Raghu had extended all kinds of support then. He had brought him to the town and consulted a doctor. He had spent quite an amount for the medicines and injections. Mayadhar recovered substantially from the affliction, though not fully. Even today, he finds it difficult to shut his eyelids fully. While he smiled or said something, the right side of the lips appeared a little crooked. A look at his face was enough to fill one's heart with grief and pathos. However, Mayadhar harbored no regrets or grief. He hardly cared for his poverty or his affliction.

Mayadhar was neither the Ward Member nor the Sarapanch nor the Chairman. He didn't own agricultural fields or a hotel or a betel shop. He was a mere insignificant, worthless, incompetent fool. Who cared whether he existed or not?

However, at the sight of Mayadhar, Raghu felt extremely delighted as if he had discovered an invaluable treasure and locked him in an embrace. "Brother, what brings you here at this hour of the day? Is everything okay? Why are you looking so run down? How are your children? Please come. We haven't met each other for long."

The two friends sat, facing each other, on two chairs in the verandah. It was a winter evening. The sky was enveloped with a thin layer of fog. Cold wind blew gently. Raghu shouted out for his wife from the verandah, "Hello, what are you doing? Mayadhar arrived just now. Please send some fried flattened-rice with a piece of ginger. Also please send two cups of tea."

Mayadhar opened his bag and took out four coconuts, some ginger and a few wood-apples. Subhadra liked this friend of her husband. Her children also respected this poor man. They all rushed out and touched his feet. They carried home what he had brought. Both the friends sat silently for some time. Raghu broke the silence and started the conversation. "Why are you looking teary-eyed? Are you crying? What is this? Tell me the truth…what happened?"

A stream of tears rolled down Mayadhar's eyes. The questioning of his dear friend induced sobs. Sticking his face into the folds of the dhoti, he burst into a loud wailing. Raghu got up from the chair, hugged him and consoled, "Listen…my brother…listen. Tell me what bothers you. We'll together try to tide over the crisis. God willing, everything will soon be okay."

After some time, Mayadhar felt pacified and the frequency of his sobs decreased. In the mean time, the snacks he had ordered for and the tea arrived. Both of them sat silently and munched the snacks. Silence pervaded the wintry night. The moon was shining in the sky, spreading its beams on the verandah. Raghu broke the silence and said, "Mayadhar, my brother, tell me what ails you. Why did you burst into a wailing?"

Mayadhar heaved a sigh and said, "Raghu, you haven't visited the village for a long time. When did you visit the *math* of lord Radhakant last?"

Raghu said, "About two or three years ago, I had paid a visit to the *math*. I was disheartened to notice that the *math* had lost its former glory and splendor. There was a time when free *Prasad* was distributed to the visitors; when there was a beeline of devotees; when *bhajans, kirtans* and celebrations including the recital of the Bhagavad Gita were organized throughout the year. The garden that once proudly displayed its collection of flowers like *baul, madhumalti,* china-rose, white tulip, jasmine, cape jasmine etc. was wallowing in great neglect. Cows, sheep and goats grazed there now. No devotee entered the *math* anymore. The entire place was as silent as a funeral ground. Pained by the sights of devastation, I have never visited it since then.

Ah, how grand and exquisite the images of the divine pair, Radha-Krishna appeared! How heavenly the black-stone image of lord Krishna appeared in his *tribhanga* stance, with a flute in hand and the yellow silk hanging down his shoulders! How charming his forehead appeared with the peacock-feather adorning it! The *kadamba* trees in the background laden with flowers and the parrots, peacocks and peahens sitting on their branches lent an astounding beauty. How divinely enchanting the glistening brass image of Radha appeared with her face glowing brightly and lips reflecting peace! The gorgeous blue saree with zari border, the crown adorning her head and the girdle around her waist enhanced her beauty. It was as if she was an incarnation of faith, love and devotion.

Who has the time, these days, to watch her beauty?

Mayadhar sat silently while Raghu narrated his experience. Thereafter, he dragged his chair towards Raghu and whispered, "Do you know brother? The images of the lords no longer adorn the sanctum sanctorum; they are missing".

"What do you mean?"

"Someone stole them day before yesterday."

"Do you know what you are saying?"

"Yes, brother! People say that Chhota Babaji has sold it to some smugglers. There is no dearth of such people in villages these days. I doubt whether the images are still there in our country; they might have exported it secretly to France or America, or to some alien land. This is premonition of great calamity for the village. Despite our presence, the village deities have disappeared. Does it matter whether we are dead or alive?"

Mayadhar broke into a sob at his own helplessness. Raghu collapsed onto his chair. He heaved deep sighs of distraught. He felt as if he had suddenly lost all his energy. After some time, he regained some strength. Mayadhar was still shedding tears. Raghu didn't ask him to be silent. Heaving a deep sigh he said, "Poor Chhota Babaji! When the *math* went through tough days, all other saints abandoned the place. There was hardly any food for them. The *Mahant* died of cancer. This Chhota Babaji was somehow managing the show. Villagers took forceful possession of the landed property of the *math*. It was difficult even to arrange some *bhog* for the deities. The rooms were demolished. Villagers had no qualms about the condition of the *math*. Instead, they carried the old bricks home. They cut and carried away the trees from the campus. Only one saint was left— Chhota Babaji. A short-heighted, emaciated, bald-headed person! He had seventeen layers of tulsi-rosary around his neck. He had a small bag hanging from his neck onto his protruding breast-bones. Most of the time, he would be found donning an old dhoti. A small ponytail adorned his head. He would move around the village, playing a pair of cymbals, and chanting the name of Gods, beg for alms.

His voice had turned weak, tired and hopeless but still he chanted, *"Hare Rama, hare Rama, hare Rama, hare hare... hare Krishna, hare Krishna, hare Krishna, hare hare."* It was he who arranged *bhog* for the lords.

About three years ago, Raghu had gone on a visit to the math. Chhota Babaji suddenly emerged from a dilapidated room, as if emerging from a hole. He clutched Raghu's hand and spoke in a pathetic voice, "I can't manage it any more. You people have remained nonchalant. The lords were the owners of three hundred sixty two acres of landed property. People have taken forceful possession of that. There was a time when *bhog* was offered five times a day. It has now become difficult to arrange *bhog* even for once a day. The silver crown that adorned the head of the image of Radha and her silver girdle were stolen by someone. No one cared to investigate who had stolen those. On the other hand, people accused me of theft. I'm the only one left to serve Him; if I leave Him who'll take care of Him? It's okay if I'm blamed in the process. Please mind one thing...the deities shouldn't go hungry ever. Many a time Radharani has appeared in my dreams telling me, "Mother Yashoda had so lovingly brought up Krishna feeding him with cream and butter. Can't the villagers offer a little milk and a palmful of rice for his *kheer*?" That day Chhota Babaji had burst into frequent sobs. How could the same person sell the images to thieves?

What does Chhota Babaji say about the incident?

Wiping his tears with the end of his dhoti, Mayadhar said, "He is absconding. Police was supposed to come to the village with sniffer dogs for further investigation. I left the village yesterday itself; I won't return to it until the images are found out".

Taking clues from what Mayadhar had said, Raghu burst out, "In that case, he mustn't have sold the images. He must have left for Vrindavan or Mathura with the images".

Mayadhar blurted out, "No...no...impossible! Do you know the weight of the idols? Chhota Babaji could never carry them alone. He must have sold them to someone and fled. Brother...this is utterly inauspicious. Evil is going to befall. Three or four years ago, when the crown and girdle of Radharani were stolen, many cows died of foot-and-mouth disease. No one knows what would happen now. The villagers are still unconcerned. That Chhota Babaji has decamped with our liver and our heart, brother".

Regional news was being telecast on the radio then. Raghu asked his daughter to bring the radio outside to him. While the radio was brought out, the second news item was being read out. Both the friends stood up in excitement and anxiety. They listened to the news carefully:

"It's reported that the images of the divine couple that were supposed to have been stolen from Radhakant Math of Kalyanpur village last Wednesday, were actually not stolen. During investigation this morning by the Superintendent of Police and other police officers, the firefighter team and police team recovered the images from a pond nearby. The team also recovered the dead body of a saint named Chhota Babaji from the pond."

Hearing this, both the friends gave out a loud moaning cry, "Chhota Babajeeeeeeeeee...

❑

(Original Odia: *Vrindavanara Sesha Dhupa*)

The Flower of the Fig Tree

Akhila Mohan Pattanaik

From the very moment her eyes fell on me, the lady presumed that I was none other than Sanjay. For some obscure reason, I couldn't protest.

Let me throw light on the incident right from its beginning.

I was, then, a post-graduate student of the Allahabad University. During the puja vacation, I had gone on a tour to Gouhati. It was a posh locality. I discovered lines and lines of tall houses with identical facades, standing gorgeously on both sides of the road. I harbored no doubt that the interiors of these houses were designed with the latest architectural marvels and fitted with all modern gadgets, guaranteeing comfort and pleasure. However, at times such indistinguishable construction creates a sense of boredom. It feels as if they have descended overnight from the pages of an architecture book and settled by the side of the road. These huge mansions lacked any distinguishing characteristics. Needless to say that I had hardly any acquaintance with the inhabitants of those houses.

Discussions about these mansions not being my prime focus, I return to the incident that had happened with me.

I was lodging in a hotel in this posh locality. One day, with evening round the corner and darkness gradually descending upon the earth, I was returning to my hotel room.

Suddenly, dark, ominous clouds appeared on the north and stormy winds began to blow. Big, silvery drops of rain began to fall. It seemed I wouldn't be able to reach my destination without getting drenched.

So, I decided to run towards the house nearby, seeking refuge. Had it been a scheduled visit, I would have been conscious of the security-man or an Alsatian dog, with natural trepidation, before opening the gate. The inevitability of getting drenched in the impending rain completely wiped out any such thought from my mind. I felt somewhat relaxed when I moved up to the verandah, just in time before the rain lashed.

The verandah was decorated in an attractive fashion. On the polished mosaic floor, four cane-basket chairs were placed. A polished teak name-plate was stuck on the front wall with a letter box just below it. A passion flower plant hung down the cement lattice on the South. A few porcelain pots proudly displayed their possessions-- some rare cacti.

It poured down incessantly. Lightning flashed in the dark sky, splitting it. Surprising! Such a huge, spacious house didn't seem to contain a single soul. The sound of a radio or the clinking of glass wares would have been out of place in such a situation but at least, someone should have displayed an urgency to shut the doors and windows. But there was hardly any noise. In the roaring wind, the thin and delicate curtains on the outer door were dancing, with their limbs outstretched. It was clearly visible, through them, that some magazines kept in the drawing room were flying delightfully in the wind. If someone had heard only the noise, he would have been compelled to guess that some pigeons had been beating their wings in a vain attempt to escape from the drawing room.

The persistent drops of rain, beating their heads on the ground, created a music that resembled the unrestrained harmony of an assortment of musical instruments emerging from the ball-room. A look at the light-post some distance away clearly showed how each water droplet pierced the one below it like a spear and got scattered like powder of silver.

A huge black limousine, entering the portico swiftly, braked. Even after its engine stopped, its headlights kept burning. I felt humiliated to the core every moment till the lights focused on me. It seemed as if I was the soldier's son, who having lost his way in the jungle, reached the demon's cave in his attempt to find a safe haven.

The lights were switched off. Darkness engulfed the surrounding within a moment.

I heard the excited voice of a lady emerging from the car. It said, "Oh...you...Sanjay!" The lady soon got out and ushered me in warmly. I saw her for the first time in the light.

She was around forty. There could be no doubt about the fact that she was extremely careful about her grooming and appearance. We kept staring at each other for some time in the light. None of us spoke a word. I was busy thinking how to tell her that she had mistaken me for Sanjay.

Without waiting for me to speak, she said, "You don't seem to have changed at all, Sanjay. You are just as I had seen you then." She summoned the cook and ordered for coffee. "I remember quite well that you didn't prefer tea. Parents remember everything about the likes and dislikes of their children. But, Sanjay, can you tell how many teaspoons of sugar I take in tea?"

Certain that my answer was going to be wrong, I preferred to remain silent. In the meantime, I marked great depths of gloom and despair engulfing her eyes. Leaning on the couch, she continued, "I know, Sanjay, it's natural not to remember things associated with us at your age. Look at Manju. I don't know what research she has been doing. Hasn't she got enough time, during the last four or five years, to meet us even once? Why can't she come when you could? Her father was telling me yesterday…he has already sent the air-ticket…look at that careless girl… she hasn't bothered to reach even though the holidays are going to be over soon."

I sat mum. Confusion was increasing every moment. I had guessed it right that unless the weather improved and it stopped raining, I wasn't going to get any respite.

The lady continued, "Manju knows pretty well that she has to leave for England this December. Her father has finalized everything. Who knows when she'll be able to meet us after that? During childhood Manju lived with me…you also lived with us…I really felt very good. But… in the name of education, one shouldn't stay away from one's own people for such a long time." Her voice and eyes reflected a sudden firmness. "I could compel Manju to come back by refusing to pay for her education for some time but as a mother, it is not expected of me."

The intensity of rain had subsided a bit. The rain-water that had stuck to the cornice fell in drops; I could hear its pitter-patter noise. I glanced my wrist watch frequently just as a hint that it was time for me to go. I said that I had an appointment with a friend; so, I would have to leave in time. When I got up to go, the lady asked me my address. I told her that I lived in Room no-24 of Hotel T-View, situated at the end of the lane. The lady perhaps was going to say something else but by that time, I had already descended the steps.

She once again stopped me. "No...you aren't going to walk in this rain." Her voice reflected the firmness of an order. "Sit in the car. The chauffer will drop you there. Besides, he'll also see the hotel."

With no other option at sight, I sat in the car. I kept my curiosities about the lady and her family in check so long as I sat in the car.

The next morning, the waiter came to the room with a hotchpotch of things. He kept those near my bed and departed. Just then I heard a gentleman knock on the door and ask for permission to get in, "May I come in, please?" I arranged my clothes and said, "Please come in."

An elderly gentleman came in. A look at him was sufficient to tell that he had been a victim to some incident terrible in nature, and as a result, he looked older. The dhoti and Punjabi that he had put on and the walking-stick that he carried showed that he was certainly aristocratic. The gentleman removed his thick-lensed spectacles, cleaned those and put those on once again. He hung the walking-stick on the chair and cast a glance at me once again.

I requested him to sit comfortably in the chair.

The moment he got into the chair he said, "I knew for certain that my wife was making a mistake. The bungalow, where you had taken shelter last evening during the rain, is mine. The lady you met is my wife. She almost compelled me to come here this morning. She is dead-sure you are Sanjay."

I begged to be forgiven and said, "Sir, my name is Ashok. I am ashamed of what happened yesterday evening. The excessive affection showered by your wife prevented me from admitting that I wasn't Sanjay."

The gentleman said, "I admit, you share astounding physical resemblance with Sanjay. A deep observation can only reveal that you are not Sanjay. However, I don't see any reason for you to beg apology or feel ashamed of anything. Ashok... this is a cruel joke by destiny. There was a time when Sanjay's marriage to my daughter Manjushree was almost fixed but unfortunately couldn't materialize.

The gentleman felt choked. He fixed his gaze on a point on the tea-poy.

In the meantime, I prepared a cup of tea and handed it over to the gentleman. While carrying the tea-cup to his lips absentmindedly he said, "It's no use telling you all that. What matters to me is that I found my wife really happy last night after a very long time. She thinks that her only dream is going to materialize soon. I don't want to wipe out her delusion. If she can spend the rest of her life happily with this harmless delusion, so be it. What more do I expect from life?"

The gentleman fell silent once again. It was as if he was talking to himself all the while. While wiping his eyes with his handkerchief after removing the thick-lense spectacles, he continued, "You are like my son. Please permit me to call you Ashok…no…no…Sanjay. I don't want to wipe out the sweet delusion of my wife by spewing the truth in some inopportune moment."

"Listen Sanjay, the only way you'll be known to the family is as Sanjay. I have something to beg you…no…no…demand you. You have to visit us at times. I never ever had any dearth of money; nor is there any dearth of it now. However, only you can fulfill the deficiency that I have."

The distress reflected in the gentleman's voice was beyond description.

"Please assure me Sanjay. Despite all your difficulties, you'll reach here at times and play the role of Sanjay."

The gentleman felt relieved as if a huge stone was removed from his chest.

"I have heard that you're leaving for Delhi by the evening flight. My wife will send certain things for Manjushree. We'll meet you at the airport. I won't waste any more of your time. I beg leave of you."

I gave the gentleman company over some distance, saw him off, and returned to my room.

In the lounge at the airport, I was anxiously searching for the mysterious couple.

Suddenly I turned back when the gentleman pressed his hand on my shoulder gently and said, "Hello, Sanjay." I was startled. By his side, stood the affectionate lady of the previous evening. She handed me over a packet, neatly packed and spoke in chaste English, "This is for Manju. Please hand it over to her anyhow."

I accepted the packet from her gladly. On the packet, with a felt pencil, only two uneven letters were scratched, "Ma-nju".

A mechanical voice requested the passengers to proceed to the air-plane.

The lady removed the gentle touch of her palm on my left hand.

I took the gentleman some distance away from her and said, "Sir, I don't know the address of Ms. Manju. It would be better if you write the address on the envelope."

I had never ever experienced two eyes of a living person becoming lifeless and still like that—like eyes of glass. His elderly body shook twice as he suppressed a seemingly loud laughter.

He brought his face closer to my ears and spoke in a suppressed voice,

"Even I don't know Manju's address. Many years ago, after my wife became mentally deranged, she died in a train accident. The news hasn't been delivered to my wife. Then Manju was a student of third year. So, after three years she must be doing research. Then, she has to leave for England for further research."

The propeller of the air-plane had started rotating vigorously, producing a loud noise. The mechanical voice was calling out my name again and again. I climbed the stairs to the air-plane. On the way, I turned my face to look at them once more. I found them waving at me.

I felt as if two friendless and cursed human-idols, two creations of a cruel God, were dancing a dance, raising their hands heavenwards.

❑

(Original Odia: *Dimiriphula*)

The Neighbour

Chandrasekhar Rath

I wonder why a person has to travel five hundred miles in a truck, disregarding the inclement stormy weather, carrying his sick children as well as all his belongings such as wooden bed, cane chairs, sacks full of things of daily use and kerosene tins. I am made to understand that at times one is compelled to travel like that. Almost everybody has had such experience at some point in time or other. Those who have never gone through such experiences, in my opinion, should have the benefit of a few. It seems, like many important and essential tasks which have remained unaccomplished, these people have failed to register one such experience. Don't you think such experiences have a beauty of their own? Such journeys have paved way for construction of roads in inaccessible areas. Besides, many strange but hitherto undisclosed facts come to the fore. In certain areas, surrounded by flood waters, sick children lose their lives in the absence of medicines and doctors. In another case a person, while passing over a culvert on a hilly-river, lost all his belongings as the truck lost balance, overturned and fell into water. He could however save himself by holding on to the wheels of the upturned vehicle and spending the night in that precarious position. Waywardness of children increases when they are shifted to new schools every two months. The rent of the houses with tiled roofs at Mayurbhanj is a bit cheaper than that of the thatched houses at Koraput.

At the end of one such journey, we reached this house.

A huge sprawling tree had spread its branches over its roof. One day or the other, it seemed, it would bend down and take the house in its grasp. Needless to mention, we were fortunate to find this house as soon as we reached the place. When we reached here it was raining cats and dogs. It was nine in the evening. Our children had fallen asleep. The surroundings looked pitch-black. The sky was covered with rain-bearing clouds. Our condition was undoubtedly pathetic.

From a distance appeared a faint light—perhaps that of a lantern. The moment we saw the light, the driver switched on the truck light. A short, dark-complexioned man came and stood by us. He carried an umbrella in one hand and a lantern in the other. He had pulled up his dhoti to the knee. The upper portion of his body had no garments. The moment I opened the door, he looked up. A stream of water ran down the umbrella. I asked, "Hello, can you show me the way to Krushna Chandra Sahu's house that has been let out to us?" He flashed a smile and said, "Sir, you are right in front of his house". He raised his left hand to point at the house.

"Oh, God! Thank you. We are saved from a lot of trouble in this darkness."

"Will you please show us the way?"

"That's exactly why I'm here, sir."

"Is it so?"

"Please follow me," said he and led us to the house.

In the truck-light the aerial roots of the banyan tree looked like innumerable pillars. The truck passed by those and came to a cart-track. Rain poured down incessantly at that time. Near a thin black door left ajar, stood that man, with an umbrella in one hand. A five feet tall boundary wall surrounded that house.

The driver applied brakes and brought the vehicle to a halt.

We shook the children out of their slumber. "Get up...children...get up. We have reached our new place." The engine was switched off; lights were switched off too. Except the light of the lantern, there was no other light in the vicinity. Rain had still not subsided. I jumped down from the truck. "Wait for some time. Let me go in first and check." I ran up to the man standing near the threshold and stood by his side. I thrust my head below the umbrella, crossed the courtyard filled with ankle-deep water and climbed onto the verandah in front of the rooms.

Not bad. Do those who live on rent have a choice? We were lucky that we got the house easily.

I asked, "Is this the bedroom?"

"Anything you wish, sir."

Not bad. The rent was two hundred rupees per month but there was no other option. In the past, houses were available on cheaper rent but not now.

"What's your name?"

"Sadhu...Sadhu Behera."

"Bah, excellent!"

"Do you have heavy things to carry in the truck?" His voice appeared strangely affable for reasons unknown. I grew suspicious.

"Not many heavy articles to carry... only three or four cots, four to five boxes, a bicycle, a sewing machine besides other essential things like a grinding stone, a pestle stone and another one for churning.

"Oh, only this much!"

What did he mean? Didn't we possess anything valuable?

"Do you think only these articles were sufficient to fill the truck? Besides, we also have a sofa set, steel materials, glass wares, books and so many other things."

"Just see how heavily it's raining now! Can anyone do anything now? Just get whatever is absolutely essential... let me go with you and help you carry things home."

A strange person...new place...rainy night...lonely house...enough to scare someone out of wits.

"There is hardly any possibility of theft here but it's always better not to take chances with your ornaments, sarees, watches and other expensive items.

"Don't worry. I'll collect all these things myself."

"Why should you get wet when I'm there to serve you? Will my master spare me if he learns about it?"

The landlord seemed to be a noble person.

Streaks of lightning shot through the dark sky. Another spell of rain followed. A feeling of restlessness enveloped us.

The stage was perhaps set for a sensational dacoity. There might even be a murder. A shiver ran down my spine.

In the faint light of the lantern, I saw a faint smile flashed on his lips.

"Master has sent food for you and for your children. I have left the food in the kitchen. Should you need, there are two umbrellas. Get the children home and eat something. Let me carry a few things home with the driver."

Food! Why should somebody send food for us? Now, there's no doubt. The food must have been laced with some intoxicant or poison. The entire family will drop dead the moment it's consumed. Then…

"No…there's no need for any food. You may take the stuff back. We'll make arrangements for ourselves."

That man still stood there flashing a smile on his lips. Only God knew knew what he was thinking.

"Will you light the hearth and cook in this rainy night? Do you want to go to bed in empty stomach? Please come to the kitchen. If you don't like the food, I'll fetch wood and water for the cooking."

He turned and entered the kitchen with the lantern.

Although emaciated, he looked strong and nimble. He could easily jump over the wall and escape after committing a crime.

The kitchen looked neat and tidy although small. In the middle of the room were kept two tiffin carriers. Beside the wall were kept a new water-pot and a clean glass.

Impossible! The whole thing appeared nothing but a huge conspiracy. Everything had been pre-conceived; only the execution remained to be done. There was no escape for the entire family tonight. My throat felt parched.

Sadhu Behera bent down and opened the lids. The fragrance of freshly rolled out *parathas* wafted out. In the other boxes were packed some *dalma* and four boiled eggs.

How surprising! How they had taken note of our likes and dislikes!

Sadhu, mind what I say! Please explain clearly what I ask you. Tell me who you are. Beware. I have a gun and a Nepalese Khukuri with me. One stroke of it is enough to rip through iron rods on this window without any harm to the sharp edges.

A perplexed Sadhu sat on the ground and looked confused. His face still reflected a faint smile. "Sir, you carry a gun with you! How wonderful! We are fortunate. Some bears are causing trouble to the villagers; if you kill a couple of those, others will disperse."

Oh, he seems too crafty and too experienced in his art! Therefore, he's showing no signs of dread or alarm.

Suddenly, I heard sound of loud footsteps floating in from outside. I grew alarmed. I thought perhaps the end had come. To my utter relief, Babuna and Buli rushed inside followed by their mother. They all had got wet and were dripping. Babuna bent down with his hands on his knees and focused his eyes on the tiffin box. "The boiled eggs look excellent; I'll eat two of these." Babuna's mother appeared cheerful the moment her eyes fell on the tiffin-boxes. She said, "You all must be feeling hungry. Sit down and eat a little each. Rest of the things can wait." Sadhu Behera gazed merrily in the direction of the children and their mother. However to my suspicious eyes it seemed as if he was surreptitiously eyeing my wife's gold bangles.

I could have shouted and prevented them from eating the food but surprisingly couldn't. My wife said, "Why are you looking here and there like a fool? Eat something, it's already too late."

Sadhu Behera looked at me and smiled. The contented eyes on his wrinkled face seemed to say, "Can you escape from the snare now?"

There seemed no escape. If he disclosed his feelings, great calamities might befall soon. If the children and their mother were told the secret that the place was a den of dreaded dacoits, they would all lose their cool. He said, "Okay then. Keep a portion for me. I'll eat later". Babuna was found gobbling up the eggs whereas Buli was wiping the *dalma* from the tip of her finger. Raising a *paratha* higher their mother said, "It feels warm even now. Just have a few bites. Do whatever you wish after that".

"No…no, I don't need to eat anything now. Sadhu, let's go and carry things home."

He sprang up to his feet immediately like a doll. He moved at a lightning speed. Bloody, rascal! Must be an expert swindler! Let me wait and watch. Am I to be deceived so easily? I've encountered many calamities in life and dealt with them successfully. Hmm…transferred to many places till now…many more to come. What do you think of me?

Both of us carried umbrellas and went outside through the courtyard.

"Hello…Rajinder," I hollered.

"Yes, sir," pat came the reply.

The Punjabi driver was a sturdy, well-built young man of forty. At the sight of him, my confidence shot up.

Even if the entire group lay in wait to overpower us, we could put up a fight. I picked up the gun from behind the seat. The moment I switched on the five-shelled hunters' torch, it focused on Sadhu Behera who was still standing beside the truck.

"Tell me, sir...what are to be carried."

I was startled. His simple innocent question confused me. I called out to him, "Listen...come here." He inched closer—a short-heighted man who looked like a black bird. "Does the landlord live somewhere nearby? He had taken so much pain to cook food for all of us; I should better visit him and say thanks for the trouble. *(Aside) I can meet your group-leaderin the process and warn him that he won't gain anything without a fight. By the way, what the name of your master is.*"

Sadhu smiled a little and said, "I don't know. I have never heard anyone call him by his name."

"In that case, how did you get the keys?"

"The owner of this house is Krushna Sahu. He lives far away from the village. He had left the keys with my master. He handed me the keys and asked me to take care of you."

His words emerged crystal clear...devoid of deception or treachery.

"Can I meet your master now?"

Sadhu flashed a smile once again. "It's difficult to meet him, that too, at this hour of the night."

"Can you point in the direction of his house?"

I focused the torch in the direction in which Sadhu

Behera had pointed his finger. I could see nothing except streams of rain pelting down.

"Sadhu...thank you very much...you needn't stay anymore. You can go now."

I looked in the direction of the driver and whispered into his ear, "It seems we are in a den of dacoits. We have to remain alert".

Ho...ho...ho...

The place reverberated with a loud Punjabi laughter. Good...this is what self-belief means. It dispelled fear. It was equivalent to displaying courage by beating the breast and twitching the moustache—the courage to deal with any eventuality head on. "Don't worry at all, sir. Let the rain subside...then we shall see." His boldness was reassuring. I got down from the vehicle and entered home without looking back, even once. Rajinder was there...to take care of everything.

The children were sitting in the kitchen after dinner. I examined their eyes thoroughly. They didn't look watery. No froth stuck to the corners of their mouths. There were no other signs of poisoning either. Oh! This was a kind of bribe then. It's easy to reach the heart through the mouth.

My wife said, "Why are you so much bothered? Eat something. We'll see what we can do in the morning. Besides, the driver is going to sleep in the truck. Come and eat a little". How fortunate I was! The dacoits had been kind enough to send a few *parathas* in my name. I leaned the gun against the wall. Three *parathas* and a bowl of delicious *dalma* disappeared into my hungry stomach within two minutes. I couldn't help appreciating the taste of the dacoits who had arranged a pot as well as a glass for us to drink water.

I'm now ready for an encounter with you tonight. Let me see what happens.

We got up and headed towards the bedroom with the children who had started dozing. The room appeared spick and span. Two mats lay in a corner. Within ten minutes of spreading the mat on the floor, the children as well as their mother went off to deep sleep. It was still raining incessantly outside. Sleep eluded my eyes. Tension kept on mounting as time passed by and night deepened.

Sadhu perhaps had fallen asleep, unwearied and unconcerned.

After I had barred all the doors, I came to a window and stood near it. I watched the rain. Perhaps they would come in groups of five or seven, donning black dresses and veiling their faces with black masks. They might be carrying iron rods, knives or even guns. Oh, what a disaster lay in wait! Had we ever brought any harm to others? Why had God devised such a plan to punish us? Why should someone plan so meticulously to loot us?

Sadhu Behera would be leading them. Like a cheetah inching closer to its prey, they would be proceeding towards the house. No...no...they weren't petty thieves; they were expected to arrive grandly. They would drive a jeep into campus, halt suddenly and jump off. Firing from their guns, they would rush towards the truck parked nearby. Keeping Rajendra hostage at knife-point, one of them would shout an order, "You son of a pig! Drive the truck or else..." He would drive the truck; why wouldn't he? The belongings loaded on the truck were mine; the truck belonged to the owner; why should he put his life at risk? Oh, that bloody traitor! In the meantime, Sadhu Behera would open the door at the back. The thieves would enter and knock on the bedroom door. The children would get up, startled; my wife would be groaning in sleep. One of the thieves would point a gun towards her and shout, "Open the door…quick…or else, I'll shoot your children on their heads." Then they would break open the door. In the ensuing melee, they would stab me on my head. They would focus the torch around and grumble, "Bloody fool! He hasn't brought anything valuable with him". The light would focus on my wife's face a little longer. Then one of them would shout directions, "Let's pick her up". Gagging her up with a piece of cloth, they would carry her like a fish. They would shove off the children. I would be lying some distance away, groaning in pain helplessly. On being kicked on their sensitive organs, the children would squirm. After sound of heavy retracing footsteps, the jeep would disappear. There would be only rain and the enveloping darkness.

Drops of perspiration appeared on the forehead. I lighted the torch but found no one around. Suddenly I heard someone sloshing in the water. The sound ran a chill down my spine. I waited with the gun ready in my hand.

Someone stood near the window silently. Instantaneously, a loud sound 'come if you dare' emerged from my mouth. When I focused the torch on the figure, I found Sadhu Behera standing there, nonchalantly and smiling.

"Oh, haven't you gone to bed till now, sir? Why are you worried? I'm keeping a watch."

"What are you doing here at this hour? What do you intend to do, you bloody traitor?"

He flashed another of his smiles. "Sir, you town

people grow very scared easily. What makes you anxious? Why are you using abusive words?" His voice appeared cool and reassuring like the voice of an acquaintance.

The hold on the gun was loosened. The loud beatings of the heart eased. I tried to moisten the lips but failed as the tongue had withered to its roots. I wanted to ask him, *"Keeping a watch? Throughout the night you'll be here? Why? Don't you have your people hiding to loot us? Tell me...Sadhu Behera...why so much concern for me...without wishing anything in return? Who instructed you to keep a watch in knee-deep water in such a rainy night? Don't you have any intentions to harm us? Doesn't your master harbor any such wishes?*

"Sir, have you eaten anything? You must be very tired. Why don't you go and take a little rest? How long would you keep standing here?" He himself was standing in the water and smiling. He was holding a small umbrella in his hand. Can such an innocent looking person turn out to be a dacoit?

I heaved a sigh of relief. I kept the torch on the ground and sat on the mat for a while.

Silence gradually deepened. My eyelids drooped. Of course, I would start and get up suddenly at times. When I shut the eyelids, my mind would be filled with ominous thoughts and gory images; when I opened them, I would find Sadhu Behera standing in front of me and smiling. Perplexed, I fell asleep, I didn't know when.

I got up with a start, only to find that the day had already broken. I found my wife having covered Buli with a corner of her saree. Babuna slept soundly with his face on the pillow.My wife said, "Listen, the child is running high temperature. She isn't responding to calls even. She is only whining".

I needed to visit the loo. I touched Buli. The temperature wouldn't be less than 105 degrees. I ran to the window, looking for someone perhaps. To my utter surprise, the truck was missing. I howled in despair. What should I do now? Where should I go? Whose help should I seek?

Four people emerged suddenly from somewhere and stood in front of the window. One of them said, "Sir, please open the door. We'll carry the belongings home".

I sat down with a thud and cursed myself. How I questioned the trustworthiness and honesty of innocent people! What had made me so weak?

Heaving a deep sigh, I opened the door. The driver was smoking his pipe some distance away whereas four people were in absolute readiness to carry things home. The truck stood close to the door.

"Where is Sadhu Behera" I asked hesitatingly. They looked at each other.

One of them asked, "Who is Sadhu Behera?"

I looked at them, dazed.

"What do you mean?"

"Oh, you mean the watchman! He wanted us to carry your belongings and left."

I wondered, "Where did he go? Why did he go?"

My wife arrived and said, "Buli had a bout of vomiting last night. I was carrying her. That man appeared and asked what had happened. I informed Buli was having fever, and asked him to call in a doctor". He went away without giving any reply. Must have gone to the doctor.

My face withered. I was now confident that he would

send for the doctor. Sadhu Behara's master was no mean a person. I wished to meet him.

The belongings were carried home one after another. The job was completed by seven thirty. The driver was ready to depart; he was only waiting for the hire charges to be paid. The four labourers were waiting for their wages.

Exactly at this time, an excellent Fiat car braked near the truck. I put on the partially dry shirt and waited to see who had come. A handsome doctor, with a stethoscope in hand, emerged from the car.

"Hello, sir. How's your daughter?"

I found it hard to control my tears. In a choked voice I said, "You, sir…I mean…a doctor…!"

"I stay in the town some fifteen miles away from here. This driver reached me very early. I know him very well. How could I say no?" He smiled and looked in the direction of the driver. What a sweet smile the driver had on his face! "His master went somewhere by train. He asked him to bring me to you after dropping him at the station."

"Who's the master? Where's Sadhu Behera?" The driver looked at me with an enigmatic smile on his face.

The doctor consoled me and proceeded towards the house. He told, "Don't worry… you'll gradually come to know everything. Why are you so much worried? Let me examine your daughter now."

The doctor had carried medicines with him. He didn't accept his fees even. He bade us goodbye with a charming smile adorning his face. I found no words to express my gratefulness. ❑

(Original Odia: *Padoshi*)

Bhola Grandpa and the Tiger

Manoj Das

B hola Grandpa lived on the western end of our village. Just in front of the hut there was a resplendent Bakul tree. It showered innumerable blossoms during the flowering season, spreading a delicate fragrance in the surrounding air. The tree was the lasting camp of a troop of monkeys. Bhola grandfather or his wife hardly bothered.

The first tale that I am going to narrate about Bhola grandpa is not based on hearsay but directly descends from experience. In the first quarter of one moonlit night, we were returning from the festival in honour of Lord Shiva. Still looked upon as a child, I had the privilege of being carried on the shoulders of the village elders.

The road was slightly long. Looked through the deep haze, it seemed as if the moon was having a bad cold. I dozed on the shoulders of the village chowkidar. My father was treated with awe and reverence and many in the crowd took it as a privilege to walk in his company. They often interjected with 'yes, sir' and 'why not' to what he said.

Suddenly, Bhola Grandpa stopped walking and burst into a loud wailing.

All were taken aback. Enquiry revealed that Bhola Grandpa had carried his grandson to the festival ground. He piloted the boy through the jostling crowd by clutching onto two of his fingers in his grip. While he took rounds of the fair ground, the child had slipped out of his grip. He hardly had any idea of it. On the way, while replying to the query of someone 'what are you holding in the grip?', he suddenly realized what had happened and burst out to a loud wailing.

On the instruction of father, two clever villagers accompanied by Bhola Grandpa, returned to the fair ground. The child had found a congenial shelter under a cow's belly and was gazing at the bustling crowd with his eyes wide open. He was rescued by the party.

I kept awake during the rest of the journey and heard father recount the following anecdote about Bhola Grandpa:

One afternoon in the past, when grandpa was young, he was found lying unconscious on our verandah, with his tongue stretched out. A shiver ran through those who found him in that condition. Later when enquiries were made, it was revealed that about an hour prior to the incident someone had broached to him a proposal for his wedding. The intensely bashful and modest grandpa stretched out his tongue. He had forgotten to withdraw it while falling asleep.

The other day, father recounted another incident related to Grandpa. While the audience looked in great expectation towards father, a bashful Grandpa was found looking down. The incident related to adolescent days of father. Bhola Grandpa was a few years older than father. One evening when it was drizzling, Grandpa confided to father and a few of his close friends that he had witnessed a group of pirates arriving the beach by our village and depositing a casket under the sand before disappearing into the sea by their dinghies.

Certain that there must be a treasure, father and his friends undertook a search for the casket in probable places. An eerie atmosphere prevailed on the deserted beach that evening as the moon hid under the patches of cloud. Besides the moaning of the breeze and the occasional sound of thunder, the only other sound was the hooting of an owl from a hollow of a dead palm tree. The search went on for a long time; the howling of a pack of jackals floating in from afar signalled that it was midnight.

Suddenly Bhola Grandpa was seen collapsing on the sand. The friends ran up to his aid. Grandfather regained consciousness. He composed himself and assured his friends that he had not been telling a lie. He confessed that the entire affair related to the pirates and the casket was part of a dream that he had that afternoon while taking a nap. Somehow or the other, he had construed it to be true.

The locale of the most memorable incident in Bhola grandpa's life was the Sunderbans. Those days, the area was impassable. Patches of deep dense forests appeared in areas surrounded by the tributaries of River Ganga. The place was the playfield of ferocious Royal Bengal tigers, besides crocodiles and poisonous serpents. Our forefathers visited these places with their men, cut down forests and converted them into agriculture lands. They even established their estates here.

During my father's time, Bhola Grandpa often went there to manage the property under our possession.

Those days, people dreaded to move around alone

even during the day, forget about the night. They always went out in groups. Despite the presence of men, each team had a necromancer. He produced a loud yell at times that was enough to immobilize any animal or spirit inimical to man. It was almost impossible to produce such a yell without proper training and practice.

That day a group of people, including Bhola Grandpa, was returning from the weekly market. He didn't remember when he was falling behind the party. He was aware of his solitariness when a Royal Bengal tiger, standing at a distance of only five yards and gazing at him fixedly, gave out not-so-loud a roar. The lean and thin Grandpa swiftly clambered up a banyan tree nearby and perched himself there. The desperate and angry tiger, annoyed at the unexpected move, circled around the tree a hundred times and sat waiting patiently for his prey to come down.

With nightfall the forest grew dark and silent. The tiger waited for Grandpa to descend. Bhola Grandpa could see the bluish-yellow eyes of the tiger. The moon walked on the sky; night passed on.

Dawn broke. Bhola Grandpa got up to the call of a pair of doves. He got down carefully. Not far away from there, on a mound, a group of Santals lived. He climbed the mound, went to the first hut, found a man and asked him a little fire to light his beedi.

The man had sat there the whole night and watched all that passed between the tiger and Grandpa. He looked at Bhola Grandpa in bewilderment for some time and then said, "Sir, you must have extraordinary powers. You walked right in front of the tiger but it only kept gaping at you. It could do you no harm. How?"

Bhola grandpa realized that he had completely forgotten about the tiger that was stalking him since the previous evening. He looked at the tree to find the retreating tiger, rendered incapacitated perhaps by helplessness, lack of sleep and bewilderment.

Bhola Grandpa is said to have passed out for a moment.

Half a century later, one morning he didn't get up from bed. He died peacefully in sleep. He was ninety-five. Nonetheless, we all bemoaned his loss. But what his octogenarian wife said by way of expressing her grief was more remarkable. "The old man must have forgotten to breathe!" she said with a sigh.

❑

(Original story: *Bhola Aja O Bagha*)

The Princess

Rabi Pattnaik

/ / You see, Mr. Mohanty, there are no more vacancies in that class. Under no circumstances, I can allow admission to your daughter. I'm extremely sorry."

Sister Joshephine Douglas, principal of the oldest and most reputed convent school of Rayapur town conveyed this in no uncertain terms. She was a Scottish national born in a Catholic family. After she had turned a nun, she came to India some forty years ago. She had been teaching in that school for the last twenty-five years.

After she had bluntly refused to entertain us, there was no meaning in continuing to sit in her chamber anymore. Many fervent appeals, requests and supplications made earlier had gone in vain. So, I thanked her, got up and left the room. My wife followed suit.

After emerging from the principal's room, we stood still for some time. There was a sprawling playground in front of us. We could hear the delighted cries of children, in school uniform engaged in different games. Perhaps my wife visualized my daughter among the children. Suddenly, my daughter pulled at one corner of my wife's saree and said, "Mommy, let's go". A few drops of tear rolled down her cheeks.

Loli was only five. Despite her tender years she understood that she wouldn't be able to read in that school. What grand pictures of the school we had painted in her mind! Over the last few months, we had constantly talked about how she was going to have new dresses, new shoes, tiffin boxes, water bottles etc. This had filled her mind with fanciful images about the school.

She was mature enough to understand that her dreams about the school were all shattered and over now. She would never be able to come to the school donning new dresses and carrying a tiffin box and water bottle. She could never get her favorite sweets and fruits that her mother had promised to pack her tiffin box with.

My wife drew her to her lap and said, "Why are you crying? What happened? See, how those small children are watching you. If they find you crying, what they would think! They would think you are afraid of coming to school. Don't cry. I'll take you to another school. That school is much better than this one. What a sweet child my daughter is! My daughter will go to a new and better school".

Loli's bitter cries didn't stop. She sobbed bitterly with her face hidden in the corner of my wife's saree. Exactly at this time, a lady who was heading towards the principal's chamber, suddenly stopped and asked us, "What happened? Why's she crying?" We were so busy consoling our daughter that we had not marked her approach. Her sudden question startled me. I looked in her direction and was startled for the second time. She was around twenty-six or twenty-seven years of age; tall and thinly built. She had a bright yellow complexion. Her dark, short, bobbed hair hung loose. Her attractive deer eyes had dark eyeballs. She had a sharp, Greek nose. Her lips looked delicate like rose petals. She had put on a synthetic georgette saree and a sleeveless blouse, both light blue in color.

I was taken aback as I was flooded with the illumination of so much beauty. I regained my composure and informed her, "She couldn't be admitted here, that's why..."

"Oh! What did the principal have to say?"

"No vacancy."

"Which class?"

'Upper Nursery or K.G would have done."

"Are you an inhabitant of this place?"

"No, I belong to Odisha. I'm a Central Government employee. I was transferred to Rayapur about three months back."

The lady remained mum for some time.

By that time, Loli had stopped crying. She was watching the surroundings dispassionately with her face resting on her mother's shoulder. The lady fondled the cheeks of my daughter and said, "No, baby no...don't cry". Then, taking both of us by surprise, she spoke to my wife in chaste Odia, "Please wait a while. Let me see if I can do something!"

With her eyes still brimming with tears, Loli looked in great disbelief the direction in which she went.

After about ten minutes, she emerged from the principal's chamber and said, "Good luck. Your child can take admission". Twitching the nose of my child she said, "What's your name, baby?" In that choked voice, she answered, "Lo....Li". "Oh! What a fine name." Loli, stop crying now. O.K., see you later. It's time for my class."

Without giving us an opportunity to express our thankfulness and gratitude, she hurriedly went away and entered her classroom.

This was how we grew acquaintance with Princess Ratnaprava Singhdeo. Within a span of two months, she became an intimate friend of my wife and a close acquaintance of my family.

Princess Singhdeo lived alone in her own palace. Palace meant a three-roomed ancient building. Years ago, her grandfather had constructed that house. When her father became a student of the Rajkumar College, this house was specially built for him. Although the house was very old, only two rooms of it had been renovated and refurbished with a fresh coat of distemper. The palace had a huge compound. A line of tin-roofed rooms existed at the back. On one side of it, there was the stable, and on the other, stood the kitchen. Beside the kitchen, there were the rooms for cooks, servants and attendants. All those rooms lay abandoned now. Even the tin-roofs had been blown away partially. The walls were covered with a thick layer of moss. A few banyan and peepul trees grew out of the cracks on the walls.

It was in that palace that the princess lived. With her lived an old maid and a cook. Adjacent to the front gate, towards one corner, a new garage had been constructed. In it was parked an ancient Austin car. She would drive the car to the town at times. When she got late or when it rained, she drove the car to the school. The princess couldn't do without the car. For her, it was a symbol of aristocracy; a reminder of her being the successor of long line of monarchs.

It's from her that we came to learn about her life history. "My father lost his kingdom when I was only one year of age. Of course, I don't remember much about those days. My nanny says, after losing the kingdom, my father grew distressed and absent-minded. Prior to that, he had taken to drinking wine but now he submerged himself in it. He hardly went out. Throughout day and night, he confined his movements to the palace. Gradually, all the assistants and servants deserted him. Friends and acquaintances renounced us. By the time I gained reason, the palace had completely lost its grandeur. Only seven or eight of us lived in the two-storeyed palace with one hundred and eight rooms. The list included my father, my mother, my nanny, I and five or six servants. All of them were more than forty years of age. I rarely met my father those days. But whenever I did, he would hold me in his lap and kiss me. He would play games with me for an hour or two. I would next meet him after two or three days.

"My father's condition forced my mother to take the rein in her hands. She tried her best to set things right. With the help of the clerks and tax-collectors, she kept accounts of agriculture, sale of paddy, sale of buildings, renting out of houses and all such affairs. How could she get enough time to spend with me? Although we were staying in the same house, I would get her company only half an hour a day. I saw her at bedtime only. After a little conversation, I would fall asleep, holding onto her tightly. The next morning, I would get up to find myself in my own bed. For me, my nanny was my childhood friend, playmate and parent.

"I was the only child of my parents. At the age of

six, I came to Rayapur with my nanny for my education. My mother felt I shouldn't attend school with the children of commoners there. Was she no more a princess simply because her father had lost his kingdom? I wouldn't allow the image of the royal family to be despoiled till I am alive."

In short, my relationship with the children of our subjects was severed from the very beginning. This old palace was tidied once again. Necessary modifications were made. The rooms were whitewashed. I, my nanny, servants, cooks, chowkidar and driver came and lived here. Out of the Austin cars that my father possessed, one was sent for my use here.

"Since that day all my relationships with my father were snapped. When I visited to our state, I would meet him for an hour or two. I missed the loving relationship that usually existed between a father and a daughter. Our conversations were limited to some banal questions like, "Are you facing any difficulties there? How are your studies going on? Read mindfully."

"Since mother was busy with so many responsibilities, she hardly got time to spend with me. She would visit me once in a month or two. Whenever she visited me, she would spend a week with me. She would never discuss anything about father; I didn't ask her anything about him either."

"The financial restrictions imposed by mother compelled father to switch over from foreign liquor to country-bred liquor. He was expelled from the inner chambers to the outer rooms. The servant attached to him would arrive both in the morning and the evening and serve him food. For months together, he and mother would hardly meet. If by chance they met, they indulged in constant bickering. Mother would lose her temper when people, who had lent father some money and supplied things on credit, arrived with long lists."

"At the behest of Ranisahiba, liquor and tiffin suppliers stopped lending him money. Rajasahib would roar like an injured lion but in the end, he would lie helplessly in that outer chamber."

"At times, I would grow compassionate with father and enraged with mother. Only five years ago that man was the most powerful person in the entire kingdom; all the subjects were shuddering in terror when he raised a finger. How wretched and pathetic a life a man, known for his courage and valor, was leading in a secluded chamber of the palace which he himself had constructed! How pitiless and ruthless the society suddenly became as if he had turned a currency out of circulation! When I ponder over the changed circumstances, tears well up in my eyes. Finally, I had to impress upon mother and make a provision of a monthly allowance of two hundred rupees for father. In the first week of every month, the Dewan would hand over the amount to him.

"You won't comprehend how profound such sorrow is; and what intense pain is caused when one's ego is shattered! If a gigantic tree is uprooted in the storm or is cut down, there is hardly any grief. But if it becomes canker-ridden; if it loses its strength and vitality day by day; and if the weevil makes it hollow and brittle, there lies the problem, the grief. This is perhaps what is meant by 'inching closer to death day by day'. I saw my own father, the unrivalled and peerless Rajasahib, inching closer to death day by day. It's good that he died; his death granted him respite from the ignominious life that he had been living. I was equally relieved of great torture and pain.

"Fifteen years after the death of my father, the system of privy purse was abolished, by Indira Gandhi. After that, Ranisahiba was compelled to change. Privy Purse provided a sense of respect to the erstwhile kings. The amount, whether it was five hundred or five lakh, was immaterial. Recognition of nobility was more valuable for them than the amount of grant. That allowance paid to royal families was a symbol of their own pride, and the last connect with their past culture and grandeur."

"Ranisahiba found herself hurled downwards—from the highest pedestal to the lowest possible step. For the first time, she realized that she was no different from other commoners and that she was standing on the same pedestal as others. She was a queen no more but another widow, like the lakhs and lakhs of widows living in this country."

"She underwent a strange transformation after that. The husband whom she had detested throughout her life; whom she had treated with the greatest disrespect and contempt towards the end of his life, suddenly looked noble and the most decent. An old and stained oil painting of Rajasahib, lying in a garbage heap in the greatest state of neglect, was recovered. It was tidied up and consecrated in a room beside her bedroom."

"Ranisahiba started revering this past memory by offering lighted incense sticks, *diyas* and oblations at the feet of this oil painting. Rajasahib turned out to be the most venerated figure for her."

"Only after the provision of Privy Purse was

abolished, Ranisahiba could comprehend the pain and distress that Rajasahib had gone through before his death."

"Ranisahiba still lives there. She has sold most of the landed property and kept the money in the bank in fixed deposits. She has sold the ancient palace to the government and shifted to a new but smaller palace on the outskirts of the town. Most part of her time is spent in worshipping God or at the foot of the oil painting of father. Even when I go there, she isn't excited as she used to be. But still, she expresses her concern for me. She would spend the entire day arranging food and clothes for me. Despite her concern, these days I mark her being affected by a sense of indifference. The shattering of her dreams has worn her out."

"After I had passed my M.A., I preferred to join this convent school as a teacher. For some obscure reason, I didn't feel like joining a college although I had been selected to join a government college. What else do I want? Do I need money? No. whatever I have is sufficient for ten people like me. Ranisahiba has set aside sufficient amounts of money for my future."

"Then, get married now."

"Ha…ha…You are speaking like my mother. Whenever I go there, she speaks about this. I have told her… if she insists on this, I would never ever come to Rajagarh."

"But why? Do you think there is a dearth of suitable young men for a beautiful, educated princess like you?"

"There's no dearth of young men but there's the dearth of a suitable prince. Can you find a noble prince for me? If you get one, I'll surely marry him."

"What do you mean? Are there no noble princes in India?"

"Certainly yes. When I was still doing my B.A, Ranisahiba was flooded with many proposals from princely kingdoms. I was the owner of immeasurable wealth. Besides, I'm beautiful, intelligent and highly educated. It's natural for them to fall for me. After the princely states were acceded into India, the princes became misguided. They turned impotent and boozers. Most of them didn't have any education to boast of. Their only goal was to get married and get a substantial dowry and lead a luxurious life. I understand…the kings had every reason to feel desperate. But why should those, who didn't know what ruling a kingdom meant, live a life of despair and desperation. I had absolutely no desire to accept the hands of a prince who didn't possess enough boldness and manliness to face the situation and establish himself by turning the tables."

The princess lovingly presents the garland around the neck of a valiant hero whom she respects, and not to an emasculated boozer and lecherous coward.

My wife found it hard to buy the last argument of the princess. She told me once, "I think there's some other secret. The matter isn't as simple as it seems."

However, in the entire Rayapur town, there was no one who spoke ill of the princess or her character. All the inhabitants were of the opinion that there was hardly any lady in the entire country who was as blameless and morally upright as the princess. There was no instance of her even having looked at young men with secret, lustful eyes. Arrogant, proud and glowing like a flame was our princess, Ratnaprava.

However, there was no dearth of people who took a great delight in staining the characters of others, falsely though.

One day my wife rushed to me with the secret information that she had got hold of from some mysterious source. She whispered, "Do you know why the princess isn't willing to get married? She maintains illicit relationship with a cousin of hers. Since she can't marry him, she has decided not to marry at all."

Oh God! What a strange creature this man is! He'll never accept that a blameless and pure person can also exist on the surface of the earth. Even, he hasn't spared you from character assassination.

In the meantime, six months had elapsed.

A new Deputy Collector came to the city on transfer. Binod Kumar. I.A.S. He was about six foot tall. Fair complexioned. Strong and well built. An attractive personality. In his conduct and manners, a manliness was discernible. He was a resident of Delhi although his forefathers belonged to Jammu. When he met the princess at our place, he fell in love with her instantaneously. After a few days, he sent the proposal from his side to marry her. I told my wife, "Ask her once and find out".

My wife after necessary consultations said, "The princess refused".

Binod Kumar asked, "Why?"

"I don't know why. She has a strange mentality. It's very difficult to discern her thoughts. Please wait for a few days; she might relent. Her heart might melt later. Is it so easy to win the heart of a princess?"

Binod Kumar waited for her to respond.

In the meantime, I received my transfer order. My wife tried for the last time before we left the place. "What's the matter, princess? Why aren't you ready to accept such a great proposal? Besides, your royal family allows grooms from different states. You speak Hindi fabulously well. In a sense, Hindi is like your mother tongue. The offer has come from his side. Without knowing anything about you, he has fallen in love with you. Why aren't you ready to relent?"

After considerable silence, the princess answered.

"Mrs. Mohanty, you won't understand. There's a constraint with princesses like me. For people like you, beauty, wealth and power count much. For me, all these considerations are insignificant. I have experienced enough of power and riches. I have also seen much of manliness and beauty. I don't know how to say. The blood flowing through your veins is red in color but the blood flowing through the veins of princesses like me is blue in color. For such a person who has blue blood, every human being irrespective of whether he is powerful, wealthy or noble minded, is only but a commoner. How can a princess disrobe herself before a commoner and allow him to enjoy her body? At least, I can't accept such a thing. I'm a princess, Mrs. Mohanty, I'm a princess.

❑

(Original story: *Rajkumari*)

The Courageous

Binapani Mohanty

The dream of a new world with its mysterious and exciting secrets always fascinated him. Despite failures, misery and disgrace coiling around his life, he found it absolutely impossible to bid goodbye to the world forever. Many a time he had subjected himself to self-condemnation; many a time he had endeavored to immerse himself fully in the sea of torture and abuses of others. However, all those inflictions had failed to stick to his heart and soul like drops of water on the lotus-leaf. Most often, he would fail to remain immersed in the gloomy atmosphere for long. His mind would soon crave for the wonders of the world. He would run after butterflies to catch them; he would talk to the pet dog and parrot; and he would be there at the table during lunch and dinner to gobble up food. If a visitor dropped in on them, he would never miss a chance to show up in his presence a couple of times. Forgetting all ills, he would switch on the radio or TV and remain glued to the programs. Only when someone reprimanded him or reminded him of his dark future, he would grow conscious of it. Unknown to him, sleep would invade his eyes. This had recurred many times...

Lying inside the mosquito net, Tipu opened his eyes. A ray of sunlight had invaded the room through a chink in the window. A sweet melodious voice floated in from the radio in the adjacent room. There was no other sound. His parents' voices were conspicuously absent.

Tipu changed sides and tried to sleep. His entire body was aching. His fingers seemed to have been detached and hands felt numb. He felt unsettled. Usually, at this time he would return home after jogging over two miles. He would snatch the cup of hot Horlicks from his mother's hands and gulp it down. These days, of course, he had started taking tea. When his father's eyes met that of his, he felt tremendously disoriented. Both of them hardly spoke a word to each other. What sort of a human being father was! He never uttered a word but the look that he gave made his blood freeze. The other day he was standing in front of the mirror and caressing his newly sprouting hair under the nose. Father was standing on the verandah and smiling faintly. The moment his eyes fell on him, he ran away. When he was reminded of that incident, he was filled with aversion for his father. However, his own existence without his father was inconceivable.

Someone was knocking on the door and calling out to him. Couldn't he sleep comfortably as long as he wished even for a day? Had he been rewarded for giving in to other's wishes for such a long time?

The voice was clearly heard this time, "Tipu! Tipu! Won't you get up today? Do you have an idea of time?" It was the usual soft, sweet voice of his sister.

Tipu didn't answer. His sister would always show off. Since the day she had joined the college, she had been showing off more. She never let him sleep comfortably either in the morning or in the evening. She had objections to his hair-style; she disapproved the way he designed his trousers. Even though she never went to the cinema, she had her ideas of the film-stars from the magazines and she expressed those openly. Father was never angry with her; he talked to her affectionately. He dropped her at her college at times too. Would the sky fall off if he talked to him affectionately or smiled a little? Earlier, mother used to stand by him when he dined and enquire affectionately if he wanted more of any item. She would give him some money to spend irrespective of whether he demanded or not. But since the day he had appeared at the Board Examination, she had been distancing herself from him too. Tipu experienced a void within. The moment he entered home, he would feel alone and hapless. Staying out would provide some respite. This condition had persisted before his result was published. Now that he had passed in the third division, the entire family lost confidence in him. Perhaps his father was well aware of his result before it was officially published.

The knocks on the door continued. He examined the string of his night suit and got up. Feeling irritated, he opened the door and rushed back to the bed once again. His sister spoke in a harsh vioce, "Hey, don't you know what time of the day it is! Your passing the matriculation doesn't mean day will be converted into night. Oh, how much you sleep these days!"

While pulling the blanket over him Tipu said, "What's the use of getting up early now? I don't have to read anything. Besides, how will I benefit from studies? Despite the best of my efforts, you know how I have been rewarded. Shouldn't I better sleep, Sister?"

"No…no…it's not okay. This time you have tasted failure; next time there might be something better in store for you."

"Henceforward, I'll never mind my studies. You know, my friends Tunu, Kalu and Chhanda have passed the examination in first divisions without ever turning the pages of their books. All I want is a seat in some college."

Unable to know how to deal with him, Sister wrinkled her brows. She further added, "Father wants you to get up early, go to market and bring vegetables so that mother can cook. The office peon won't come today. Mother gets irritated everyday as he gets late. Can't you leave bed early and get the vegetables from the market?"

"I'm sorry, I can't help. You people may decide not to serve me in return. What will people say?"

"Worried about self-respect? If you were concerned about it, you wouldn't have passed in the third division. What great hopes father had! You are the elder son… by the time Bapu writes his examination, father would have retired."

In the meantime, sister had removed the mosquito net and was looking curiously at Tipu's bandaged heel. Tipu knew he had to provide some explanation. He wondered what he would say. When he was returning home after the results were announced, he stepped into a pothole and received a minor injury. He was readying himself to run and jump into River Mahanadi when some of his friends intervened and prevented him from doing so. He had decided not to return home with his face stained like that. Had he been successful in his attempt yesterday, he wouldn't have been made to face the disgrace of getting up early and going to market.

Tipu hadn't met his father face to face since the last evening. His mother didn't have much opportunity to see how he had injured his leg. Otherwise, she would have raised much hue and cry. Nobody expressed concern unless he faced a big accident. Only this sister of his was relentless. She poked her nose in his affairs and derived much pleasure when he was insulted. Tipu wanted to say something but restrained himself. He got up. He looked at his sister and understood why she was angry. He came out with his shirt on.

He found his mother coming out of the bathroom. Her eyes looked red and face appeared swollen. His father sat on the outside verandah with the newspaper in his hand. Surprisingly, he discovered the office peon standing at one corner in a supplicating posture. His sister was a habitual liar. Why did she tell so many lies every day?

The peon said, "Brother, let's go quickly. People must have bought their quota of the fish already. The stock would be exhausted if we don't reach there early. Besides, mother would be angry if we have to pay extra."

Tipu said angrily, "Why are you waiting for me? Do I ever accompany you?"

"I…I…do you think…?"

"Go with him. Nata will show all important places. You'll have to go to the market all alone from tomorrow," said father in a voice flushed with anger. Tipu asked, "Why do I have to go to market?" Father replied, "What would you do sitting at home? With the marks you have scored, you won't get a seat in any college. I don't have money enough to send you to some college on donation. Besides, I have to take care of the two marriageable daughters.

Enough is enough. Take care of household affairs so that I get a little respite."

Mother wiped her tears and went towards the kitchen. Elder sister was visible nowhere. Younger sister had suddenly disappeared. When father got angry the entire house appeared barren. Suddenly, an unknown personality raised his head from within Tipu. He had read class three onwards on scholarships, without being a burden on his father. His father was proud of him on account of that. He had tried his best to pass the matriculation examination with a good score. He was terribly disappointed and hurt with his marks. What hurt him more was the fact that no one in the family was compassionate with him for his undesirable failure. It's true that some of his friends had scored better than him and secured first divisions. But no one had the time to ponder as to how they were able to secure such good marks. They were only interested in accusing him and offending him. What insults they heaped on him! He expected a little sympathy from his father. Did his failure to secure better marks mean he would bid goodbye to his studies and buy groceries and vegetables like a servant?

While walking away from the spot, hand in pockets, Tipu said, "I can't go the market to buy groceries and vegetables". Flinging the paper from his hand onto the ground father said, "What else can you do? Do you know your worth in the market? You are worth nothing. From now onwards, take care of yourself. I had hoped that you would read well and make a man of yourself. You have betrayed the trust I had put in you." Tipu retorted, "Father, it's true that I have secured a third division but that doesn't mean I'm worth nothing. I can confidently tell you that my answer scripts have not been evaluated properly. If the scripts had been evaluated properly, the foundations for a future I.A.S. officer would have been laid. I understand it didn't happen that way. Does it mean that I should have grown nervous and hanged myself to death or jumped into a pond? Just believe me; I haven't lost my faith in myself."

Father looked into Tipu's face in wonder. His conviction in himself had staggered a bit. This was the right time to disappear from the spot. Tipu left the front room and came out to the verandah. That his father's dream of making him an I.A.S. officer was spoiled, he was hardly responsible for it.

He seethed in anger. How could he stay at home under such circumstances? Better if he took to the streets. What sins had he committed? Why should he be punished without committing any offence?

He walked hurriedly among the crowd in the street. Nata came from behind and brushed past him. At the sight of him, he felt startled. Perhaps Nata had come to take him back home. Perhaps mother had grown worried, quarreled with father and sent Nata to get him back. But Nata didn't stop. He went past him and entered the market. A deep sigh of disappointment and despair escaped his heart.

Tipu's eyes suddenly fell on the Headmaster of his school. While purchasing potatoes from the market, he was looking at him through the corner of his spectacles. Tipu felt as if an electric current passed through him. How many times this brute had mocked him! Intentionally, he would deduct marks. Once he had borrowed his expensive pen but didn't return it. Despite being quizzed at home and condemned for his irresponsibility, Tipu didn't open his mouth. He was after all his teacher. He had been awarded by the President for being an excellent teacher. Tipu's palms automatically joined together in 'namaskar'.

The headmaster spoke in a solemn voice, "Hey, boy. All others came to school after the result was out and saw the list. I was told that you were doubtful about the list published here and so you went to Cuttack to verify your result. What did you find?"

"Sir," said Tipu, his voice angst-ridden.

"Let it be so. How do you care? You don't care because you are a rich man's son. Do whatever you wish but in this competitive era if you aren't careful about your career, you'll spoil everything. Money has spoiled you, son. Otherwise, despite the efforts of three tuition teachers you would not have faired so poorly. Fie! Fie!"

Tipu grew absentminded. Unlike other students, he hadn't lost his cool in the examination hall. He knew answers to all questions and attempted them unwearied. When the headmaster was moving around the examination hall, he didn't even stop near him. Tipu failed to understand where he lost so many marks. The headmaster's accusations made him bleed. He angrily answered,

"Sir, I was ashamed of my performance and therefore I had left for Cuttack. I wasn't afraid of you. You accused me of performing poorly despite the help of three tuition teachers. You have perhaps forgotten that those three teachers work in your school."

Having burst out thus, Tipu left the place and walked away. However, his heart shuddered for a moment at his own impudence. The next moment he comforted himself. Were they such men of learning and scholarship that one shouldn't argue with them? Why should he bend down his head in respect before them when they don't lose an opportunity to mock at him?

Strangely, his heart felt very light today. As if there was nothing inside; as if a void engulfed his inner being! How come the entire world had become so insensitive! Wouldn't anyone sympathize with him? Would he only be the victim of their mockery? Unlike his classmates, he had never ridiculed others; he had never threatened others through anonymous letters; he had never ever created a feeling of derision in others by unnecessarily indulging in arguments with them. Still then, everyone starting from the members of his family to outsiders treated him with disdain. He failed to comprehend what steps he should take to mitigate his suffering. He had lost his confidence in himself since the previous evening.

Tipu found himself standing in front of his friend Shekhar's house. So many times in the past Shekhar was angry with Tipu for not visiting him. Many times he had shed tears before Tipu saying that he was staring straight into a dark future as he was neither a good student nor a rich man's son. Surprisingly, the same Shekhar had passed in the second division whereas Tipu had passed in the third. Why? When Shekhar carried incriminating materials in his pant pockets or stuck to his thighs he would never look nervous. On the other hand, Shekhar's carrying those to the examination would make Tipu so uneasy that his pen would refuse to move. What value did his honesty have? Everybody had expected him not only to pass in the first division but also stand among the best ten rank holders, but their hopes were dashed to the ground.

Lost in thoughts about his own troubled life, he stepped on the stairs of Shekhar's house. Suddenly he was distracted by someone's voice. "Why did you stop here, son? Are you afraid of entering a poor man's doors? I am happy that Shekhar passed with distinction; I had been to the temple to pay obeisance to God. Please wait; the boy is still sleeping."

Tipu turned back and found Shekhar's mother looking at him with the love-filled soothing eyes of a mother. On the other hand, he was reminded of the swollen downcast eyes of his mother. His inside writhed in excruciating pain a few times. Like an automaton he blurted out, "I have come to congratulate Sekhar. I haven't seen him since yesterday."

"Shekhar was sad for you. Despite being a good student..."

Bringing an abrupt end to her remarks Tipu said, "I beg leave of you, Aunt. Let Shekhar sleep. I'll come to meet him later."

"It's okay son. He returned at two in the morning. A lazy fellow, he usually gets up late. It's his good luck that he is climbing higher in the ladder of success... you can come sometime later."

Shekhar's mother went in, almost pushing aside Tipu on the way. She didn't want to shatter Shekhar's peace by waking him up so early on a day like this. It's true that he wasn't a good student but his results spoke a different story.

Tipu once again came to the main road. Nowhere did he find even an iota of peace or tranquility. Everybody including his family members and acquaintances looked up to him in eyes of contempt. Had Tipu lost his right to live? Wasn't there any difference between whether he chose to die or to remain alive? It was better to bid goodbye to the world before being branded a 'useless incompetent fool'. Why should he live to lead a disgraceful life? Death was a thousand times better than such a contemptuous life. He will surely commit suicide. This was the only way to prove others that he didn't care for them too. He had lived in this world on his own terms; he would bid it goodbye as and when he wished. The pitiable result in the examination wasn't the sole reason. If people underestimated him without valid reasons, he could give them a befitting reply. He was scared of none.

Tipu rushed ahead. No... he wouldn't think of remaining alive in this hostile world anymore.

After about ten minutes of walking, he gasped for breath. Streams of sweat ran down and drenched his body. He was feeling hungry too. When he slowed down his pace, he felt as if someone was calling him by his name.

Tipu somehow dragged himself from the main road to a narrow alley. Small narrow lanes, dilapidated buildings, small shops on both sides of the roads greeted him. His attention was suddenly drawn towards that boy sitting on an old bench in a shop. That boy...he would sport dense-grown locks at times and a bald head at others...only last year when they were in the same class, police arrested him on suspicion... he bore a funny name...Ladukeswar. His pet-names were 'Ladu,' and 'Ladia'. He was released from jail after five months. Tipu met him once after he had returned from jail but the red hot eyes with which he looked at Tipu, made him stagger. Tipu left the spot without saying him anything. But today...

Ladu was perhaps eating something from a leaf bowl. The moment he saw Tipu, he flashed a peculiar smile and said, "Hello, you rich man's son! How come you appear in this disreputed street of ours? Suriya told me you had passed."

Tipu failed to remember who Suriya was. Unknown to him, his eyes were glued to the leaf bowl that Ladu held. Ladu stopped eating, got up, came near him, rested his hands on the latter's shoulders and said, "Hey! Why are you eyeing my plate like this? Are you hungry? Do you want to eat *bada*s and curry? We don't have any porcelain plates here... (smiles). Tipu informed him, "It's true that I am feeling hungry but I don't have any money in my pocket." Ladu dragged him by his hand, made him sit on the bench and said, "Don't think I can't spare a little sum like fifty paise or a rupee for a friend. Tell me, why do you keep up such an appearance? Have you left home? I know you rich man's children very well. You can crumble very easily. You people believe in only one thing. Life must pass smoothly. If there's a small trouble, you would either commit suicide or leave home forever."

Tipu gobbled up one *bada* after another from the leaf bowl that the shopkeeper had given him. He was surprised to think how Ladu got a whiff of his inner suffering. The young man, whom everybody made the butt of their accusations and wounded his heart with words like 'thief,' 'goonda,' 'despicable,' 'malicious' etc., was compassionate towards him and gave him food when he was hungry. He might be a goonda and a malicious character but he bore a heart that felt for others. Even if he ridiculed him, he would tolerate everything without protest. After eating the *bada*s and drinking some water, he felt a little perked up. He spoke in a regretful voice, "Friend, I'm sorry. I had misunderstood you. Please pardon me. Today I realize you have a noble heart."

Ladu got up from the bench, stretched out his hands a couple of times in the manner of doing some exercise and said, "Nonsense! Stop this heart business. I regret to tell you this. When I was sent to jail, none of my friends was compassionate towards me. However, I don't care at all what they all feel about me. So long as I have the support of my hands, I'm not scared of anything or anybody."

What a courageous boy Ladu was! He hardly gave a damn to anything or anybody. Why wasn't he like him? Is it possible to become one like him?

Lady stopped doing the exercise, clutched Tipu's hand and said, "Let's now go to our house".

Tipu shrank a little within and said, "No...no...not today. Maybe some other day!"

"Oh! I understand. You are afraid, aren't you? Someone may find out. Then they may despise you for being a thief and a rascal's companion."

Tipu got up without showing any reaction. He spoke in a whispering voice, "I'll come tomorrow and pay you back your money. Let me go now..."

Tipu couldn't complete his statement. A strong slap landed on his ear, shattering his eardrum. He collapsed to the ground, almost senseless. Ladu was heard saying, "You bloody fool...you plate licking cur...it's for people like you that the country is heading for a disaster."

When Tipu regained consciousness, he found himself lying on bed at home. His teary-eyed mother was caressing his feet. His worried father was moving to and fro with his hands in his pocket. Tipu couldn't look into his eyes. He shut his eyelids. His father might get angry and take him to task. He heard his father say, "Please don't make me distraught by crying like this. A child like this is fit to be disowned. How shameful! He has become friends with thieves and murderers!"

Mother stopped sobbing on father's instruction but said, "Only for you…only for you things have come to such a pass. When Ladu was sent to jail without any proof against him, didn't I advise you not to accuse another person's child baselessly. Didn't I tell you then if we accuse an innocent child today, tomorrow someone might accuse our child? Look, how he decided to take revenge. Nothing will happen to him for sure, but our family name will be tarnished." Father roared, "Shut up…I've no time to listen to your nonsense. Take care of your son. He's going astray. If you don't, he will emerge as the second Ladukeswar. Before I see that happen either he should embrace death or I. Fie! Fie!"

Father left the room in a huff. Mother moaned, with her head on Tipu's feet, in an exasperated voice, "Hey Tipu! If you don't mend your ways, I'll drink poison and die."

Tipu lay there as if turned into stone. He could hardly recollect what had happened with him. He was not even able to portray anyone's face clearly in his mind's eye.

But one thing was certain. He understood he was the sole reason for this breach of peace. Waves of pain created great turmoil in his heart. He had been swimming relentlessly in the water. No matter how much he tried for an escape, his attempts ended in failure. The shore was hardly visible. The conflict that went on in his mind over the last few days had made him restless and wearied. Will he lose the war?

No…he wouldn't be able to withstand so much pain. He would leave everything and go away. Unimaginable pain shrouded the very birth of human beings; to sustain oneself in this world, one had to endure more pain. He wouldn't be able to fit into a wrapper; he wouldn't mug up lines from books and sit in the examination hall. He would go far away where no one else could reach-where nobody would recognize him; where nobody would constantly warn him about his actions; where nobody would wish to see him different from other human beings. He would merge into humanity there.

Tipu was feigning sleep while waiting for the deep silence of midnight. The ticking of the wall clock sounded like heavy crashing of boulders to his ears and heart.

❑

(Original Odia: *Sahasi*)

The Banquet

Pratibha Ray

Banquet...to be hosted by the wealthy master... celebrating a marriage in the family! Guests, as usual, were expected to eat less and leave greater portions on the plate untouched. There the real fun lay.

The dinner was to be laid out on the evening of the marriage but meticulous preparations had been going on for a fortnight. With hunger written all over his face, the boy frequented the place in expectation of sumptuous dishes. Even though no one wanted him in particular, he was there at everybody's beck and call. Workers had been working overtime to tidy up the nearby field, mow the grass, erect poles and put up the tent. The child ran errands without expecting any wages. He didn't feel repentant either. He was no less enthusiastic than the members of the celebrating family. It was as if someone from his own family was getting married. The sooner the work was over, the dinner would be hosted and he would get his share of the leftovers. The possibility of licking the used plates of guests filled his emaciated, reedy legs with a strange sensation.

These days, the used plates are no more discarded

on the road beyond the tent. They use drums to collect the garbage. The child had the uncanny knack of scrounging out pieces of leftover fish or mutton from it. Some others discarded the used plates near the drains. The child hardly dreaded the drains. Were children like him in any way better than worms in the gutters? He dreaded only the street dogs. If by chance he came on their way, there was bound to be a fight. A hungry dog is mightier than a hungry man. Besides, man's teeth are not as sharp and vicious as a dog's. This deficiency often made the child distraught. The street dogs behaved as if they were mighty kings and the street children were their poor subjects. The wretched children were allowed to enjoy their share only after the kings had their fill. While the dogs happily gobbled up the food, the children helplessly looked on. A dog could bite a human being and not the vice versa. However, this game had made the child an expert in the field of scrounging for food.

In a few days, due to the efforts of the indigent workers, the meshy field was transformed into a tidied-up place. If the wretched people or their soiled hands refused to slog, who would clean the heaps of garbage and filth?

The feast was to be served at night. Since morning, smoke had started billowing out of the makeshift kitchen. The aroma of dishes had already spread in the air. Through the nose and ears, the savory smell entered the veins, arteries and entrails. Like gushes of flood water, the child's mouth watered. Rich people treat themselves to delicious dishes in their homes or under the tents, of course away from the sights of the poor. Why do they allow the aroma to be drifted away by the wind, tormenting the latter?

The wealthy are generous in the sense that they never leave the plate clean. They leave a portion for the poor. Their dogs are not served with the leftover food. "The dogs take offense," they say. Like their master, the dog even leaves a portion of the food untouched. It never has to go hungry. So, it never feels the need to look for leftover food. On the other hand, hunger makes the poor apathetic. Had it not been the case, he would feel offended to touch the leftover food and prefer to die in hunger.

The child kept himself as close to the tent as was possible, like a greedy cat. After long, he was going to entertain himself to the savory taste of delicious dishes. Did it matter if it was someone's leftover food? The term 'leftover' never divested the food of its taste. The sweetness of the pudding hardly diminished: the sour tasting dishes hardly tasted different. Why should food be tainted for no fault of its own? When the street dogs and wild cats entertained no such thoughts, why should a human child harbour one? How were street boys different from street animals?

At the fall of night, there arrived many wealthy couples, donned in gorgeous clothes. The boy in rags shrank a little at the sight of their clothes. It was difficult to distinguish those who accompanied the bride from those who accompanied the groom. All of them carried some stuff wrapped in blue and red packets. Those contained presents for the newly-weds. No guest usually visits a marriage pandal without gifts. Although the boy was voluntarily rendering help, he was lucky that no one had invited him to the dinner. No presents were required to lick the leftover dishes. Otherwise, he would have been in grave trouble. Where would he have brought money from to buy gifts?

Three or four women, dressed in gorgeous sarees, stood at the entrance. They accorded the guests a warm welcome. When the guests reached the bride and bridegroom on the stage, one person collected the gifts from them and like an accountant, carefully noted down their names and addresses. The boy was happy that he had no money in his pocket. Otherwise, he would have arrived with a gift. The accountant-like person would have noted down his name and address. Later, they would have calculated the value of each gift and the per-head expenditure to evaluate whose worth was more. Besides, just when the guests were ready to throw lumps of food into their mouths, the photographer would flash his light on them and click their photos. Fie! Fie! What would a person do in taking photos and keeping track of how many lumps of food a guest had?

Oh! When will they dispose of the used plates? The child was feeling sleepy by then. The delicious aroma of dishes had long stimulated his hunger. The fire of hunger burnt brightly. The street dogs, in anticipation of their share, had already started crowding the place beyond the boundary wall. Strangely, sleep eluded the dogs but human beings felt sleepy.

Why was there so much delay? Perhaps there was no one to collect the used plates and dispose those of. He had already worked so much without being asked to; what harm was there if he collected the used plates himself? Conversely, this act of his could make the master happy. There was but one problem. How could a boy in rags visit a neat and tidy place or go near the sophisticated gathering?

Taking advantage of the crowd, the boy sneaked in and hid under a serving-table. After the batch of guests had finished eating, he would emerge from under the table, pick up the used plates, and eat the leftover food before falling asleep. He felt immensely tired after the day's hard work. The dogs had done nothing but were ready to claim their share. It would be wise for him if he collected the used plates with the leftover food before the dogs could lay siege on those.

The servers were serving dishes—pudding, pulao, purees, rasogollas, fish and mutton. Let him put on the plate as many pieces of each as he wanted. There was nothing to worry if the guest failed to eat all. He would enough for tonight, tomorrow morning and also for the evening. He hardly cared if the dishes were freshly cooked or if they had been cooked some other day. "Mr. Server... serve more food onto the plate. This is the banquet hosted by a wealthy man. Don't worry about the expenses...why are you serving only a small quantity of everything?"

The boy's mouth continued to water. Sugar syrup from the rasogollas seeped through the chinks in the planks of the table. He heard the ladies and gentlemen say, "No, No...not any more. No sweets please...no pudding please." He felt irritated. Who in this world refused to have more of pudding, purees, fish and mutton? He hadn't heard anything of that sort since the day he had gathered sense. The wealthy were masters of pretense. How could they say 'no' to everything? Why did they come to the banquet then? Just to show up their wealth?

"It's okay. If you aren't interested in eating anymore, please leave the table." The eagerness of the boy to collect the used plates had reached its zenith. He got up to pick those up. At the sight of him, the faces of the guests wrinkled. They frowned in disdain. How dare the worm of the gutter reach as far as the dining table? The attention of the neat and tidy server was diverted towards the boy. He yelled 'get out' and dragged him out of the hiding place. The faces of all the guests, enjoying the sweet pudding, suddenly turned sour. They all behaved as if a foul stench had spread everywhere. An unknown person ran threateningly towards the boy. He struck the boy on the back of his head a few times and drove him out of the place. The boy broke into a sob. He felt hurt, not by insults heaped on him but because of the blows landing on his back. Poor children don't mind abuse; only the blows are physically hurtful.

The hungry boy wailed for a long time. It was almost midnight. He decided to search for the discarded plates in the morning and have his fill. He fell asleep. Dreams disturbed him. He dreamt he was partaking in the dinner and savoring the delicacies.

By the time he got up in the morning, he found that the rascal curs had licked the plates clean, so clean that they resembled bald heads. The banquet being over, the tents were being removed. The utensils of the caterer were being loaded into a vehicle. Someone shouted, "Hey, boy! What are you gaping at? Come here. Lend a helping hand. Don't you know? There is a feast tomorrow in the next lane."

The child started carrying all utensils including ladles and spoons one by one to the man on the vehicle. Soon, he was seen running after the vehicle like a calf after its mother.

❑

(Original story: *Bhoji)*

Gopapura

Ramachandra Behera

Every time he reached home these days, some disaster would welcome him, with its arms outstretched. Notwithstanding his humble prayers to God, the lemon tree shed its immature, green lemons as if it went through an abortion. The plantain spike was so large that the prop couldn't hold it. The entire tree was found leaning on the roof in a few days. The other day he came to learn that the silver pan had worn out and developed a hole. The yoke that he had purchased a few days ago broke into two. The pumpkin plant was gasping for breath, as if it had given up its desire to live.

Many of these disasters were neither unprecedented nor unnatural in human history. So, when one encountered those, there's hardly any need of searching for some hidden message. Many such tragedies occurred in life. Maybe, one day their magnitude would be beyond one's capability to absorb. Then everything would go topsy-turvy.

However, there was no justification in harboring such thoughts. Why shouldn't such trifles befall during the life's journey? No...no... he wasn't singled out for ill-treatment. The lemon tree in Abhiram's backyard was also reduced to its skeletal remains. Almost every other day someone's plantain tree leaned on some support; their newly-procured yokes were untimely damaged.

No, there's nothing much to be worried about. The fields were expected to yield good crops this year; the progress and promise that they exhibited at the end of October was at least satisfying. He hadn't expected that the cow, which had borne a calf for the first time, would give so much milk. The couple of bullocks looked strong, sturdy and healthy. Weren't these remarkable to note? Didn't the small disasters pale into insignificance when compared to good things happening in life?

He had carried a few bundles of grass on the carrier of his bicycle. His bag hung from the handle. Before reaching home, he stopped to buy a few items of grocery from the village-shop.

While continuing to wipe his face, Nirakar once again had a satisfying look at his fields. A delightful green color was sprouting out of the earth. Perhaps the boundary ridge wouldn't be able to contain so much wealth. The ridge was sandwiched between overgrowing grass on it and abundance of rice paddy plants below. Not only his own fields but the fields all around promised plenty of harvest and a secure future for their owners.

But when he reached home, he felt as if the citadel of security had already crumbled. What he had to face wasn't a mere landslip but a great disaster that had the intensity to smash everything to dust. If immediate steps were not taken, everything that he was proud of -- his robust physique, the green fields, the milch cow and the sturdy bullocks, would turn irrelevant and useless. Sumitra, his wife, had been dealing with, fearfully and anxiously, their five year old child for the last one hour. Nirakar came and leaned the cycle against the outer wall. The grocery items and bundles of grass were still hanging on the carrier and handle. The deep breathing of the bullocks and the peeing sound of the cow couldn't distract him. Standing near the threshold he said, "Hello! What's the matter? Why is everything so silent today?" The glass cover of the lantern that had already grown half-black with soot, was desperately struggling to light the verandah. An eerie silence spread in the entire house including its ceiling, kutcha walls and cemented flooring. Dim-light and illness increased his worry. In addition, the silence of the child and his mother was too bothersome for him. Usually, at this time of the evening, the woman remained busy in the kitchen. Besides, the big cauldron would lie in the courtyard; remnants of rice-husk mixed with rice-water would still be left for the cattle to drink.

"What's the problem?" asked he, demanding an answer. He touched the forehead of the ill-child with his palm. In the dim light of the room he could see two eyes opening slightly and a tongue licking the lips. Only the heaving of the chest suggested that the child was alive.

When he looked at Sumitra, he saw that she had her look fixed on him. She appeared unshaken and steady as usual. This quality of her made Nirakar firm and confident to deal with things. She was different from others' wives in this respect. She was never prone to feeling desperate; she never made others feel helpless either. She would neither become impatient easily nor make another feel exasperated.

Sumitra knew she had to offer an explanation to him. "This morning, he seemed to have caught a cold. You had seen it yourself. At about twelve or one in the afternoon he said he was feeling a little cold. He was shivering. By then, the temperature had shot up. The temperature has been shooting up since then; it isn't showing any sign of subsiding."

Nirakar looked all around and grew absent-minded. He needed a way—a way that would lead to a solution. "Why didn't you ask Arun to pay a visit? I was working in the field. At least, you could have sent me a message." Then he spoke in a manner of addressing himself, "It's already night. What can be done now?"

"Arun did come," Sumitra continued giving an account of herself. She further added, "He gave some medicines. Surprisingly, the homoeopathic medicine prescribed by him proves ineffectual in case of this boy. He told me the child would get well. I asked him to pass the information to you. He agreed to send you the message. I also asked a few others going your way to pass the message to you. How could I go anywhere leaving the child alone in the house?"

Nirakar cast another quick look around, looking for a solution. He didn't seem to have an immediate solution to the problem at hand. While he worked in the field, illness shrouded his child with its veil."

"Should we carry him to hospital?" He wasn't very firm about the idea that he himself had floated. This he didn't say to elicit an advice from Sumitra either. Perhaps it would be better if the child was carried to hospital. This statement of him was reflective of his inner conflict and helplessness.

"Why don't you go to Arun once again for advice?" Sumitra proposed.

"What would I ask again? He is inexperienced. He was a good student but couldn't achieve anything worthwhile. He consults homoeopathic books and prescribes medicines. Is he expected to have an in-depth knowledge of things? He has already paid a visit. What else can he do if we pester him?"

He reached the window. In a voice ridden with conflict he asked, "Why didn't you ask Arun why the child was suddenly taken ill like this?"

"I asked him. He said it was a mere case of fever. It would subside with the passage of time."

"The fever will subside," Nirakar reassured himself. How long did the fever usually take to subside? Besides, he had taken medicines. The thought made him feel reassured. If it was fever, there was no need of feeling disoriented like this. He looked at the child, running high temperature and lying with his eyes closed. He dare not touch his forehead. What would he do if the temperature had gone up further? Nirakar wondered if his village that consisted of twenty-five to thirty thatched houses had a solution to such a problem.

The terrifying moment came at about ten in the night. Sumitra was busy placing a napkin dipped in water on the child's forehead hoping that it would help the temperature to subside. She abruptly stopped. She saw the child having hiccups. His tiny body was having convulsions. He had opened his eyes for a second but she wasn't sure if he had seen anything. The eye-balls reflected a restless motion. The eyelids drooped down and covered them soon.

"What shall we do now?" Nirakar's voice appeared pathetic and restless. Sumitra's muscles contracted, ready to face the debacle. They remained gazing into each other's face for quite some time.

"We shouldn't make any further delay." Nirakar remarked. "We have to carry him to the doctor. Can't tolerate to see him writhing in pain anymore."

While changing her saree, Sumitra expressed her doubt, "What shall we do in case the boatman is absent? How shall we cross the river and reach the other bank?"

This question had the ability to paralyze the fingers busy buttoning the shirt. The river was some two kilometers away from the village. On the other side, there ran a narrow road full of stones and potholes. This road had existed despite being subjected to long neglect. Two or three villages lay by roadside. One had to negotiate the bumpy road on his cycle. The National Highway was about five kilometers away from the other bank. One would come across a black-topped road upon touching it. This road led to the District Headquarters hospital. It wasn't that far from the village; only eleven or twelve kilometers away from there. The distance seemed much because of the huge river that flowed in between.

"Why wouldn't the boatman be there?" said Nirakar laying some unnecessary stress. Of course, he himself wasn't confident about this. "People cross the river even at midnight. The boatman sleeps in a hut on the bank."

Carrying a few things in a bag, they locked the door and came out to the street. Nirakar brought the bicycle. Sumitra carried the ill-child on her bosom and a torch in her hand.

This was a repetition of the experience they had about one and a half years ago. That day it was about eleven in the morning. Now it was about eleven in the night. On that occasion, the condition of this child had grown so worse that a strong lady like Sumitra had broken down. Nirakar had lost all his hopes. They reached the doctor's quarter. The doctor wasn't satisfied with the medicines and injections that he himself prescribed. He wanted stool and urine examinations to be carried out. After the results came, he prescribed some more medicines. Oh, what troubles he had to undertake on that occasion! However, the consolation was that the result of the hard work and expenses was visible after three or four days. The problem they faced today was to cross the river and reach the hospital at this hour of the night.

Nirakar pressed the paddle. Sumitra sat on the carrier with the child. She would press the switch of the torch showing some light whenever she could. On both sides of this narrow road hedges grew, with their branches hanging on to the road. They would turn brown in a month or two and lose their leaves. They would look bare and battered till the rains came next. The entire Earth, barring the wheels of the bicycle, appeared to have become still. The moon that looked like a mirror without the layer of mercury hung on its heavenly bower. The tranquil sky with its panoply of stars looked down peacefully. It was as if everything had stopped moving.

The bicycle was constantly moving forward. Of course, the moaning of the child would break his concentration at times. At times, he would feel proud of his and Sumitra's strong and stout physique. If given two spades, they could dig a tunnel from the surface of earth to hell. They could even make the surface of the earth plain. For hours, they could supply water to the fields. They could plant paddy till the distant horizon. They could collect all the paddy bundles and stack them in the backyard. But look at the child born of them. The poor boy was perennially ill with cold or fever.

They had to get down on reaching the river-bank; they couldn't ride the bicycle from there till the river. They had to negotiate a descent. Whether it was a bicycle or a scooter, one had to walk till the river. The hut in which the boatman took rest was open from all sides. The roof was made of a few palm leaves. There lay a wooden cot with its legs buried into the sand. The boatman managed his business from here.

Sumitra switched on the torch and focused on the cot. The cot lay abandoned. As if it lay outstretched after the day's hard labor! Was the boatman up to some trick to fleece more money? Nirakar searched below the cot. He focused the torch as far as its light reached. There was no body in the vicinity. The palm leaves were swaying in the breeze.

Their throats felt parched. The river flowing nearby couldn't moisten these. Their hearts pounded heavily. They felt constricted by a sense of distress and desolation. Wherever they turned their faces, they found inadequate facilities infesting their lives. The child's illness was gradually turning more and more serious. The frequency of hiccups was going up. The boatman had fled abandoning his post. The river flowed dispassionately. It seemed as if it was in no hurry. Its firm and unsteady flow indicated that if they had mastered the tricks, they could cross it easily. If they didn't possess the necessary mastery and if the method they selected was flawed, it shouldn't be faulted with for any disaster. Remedy for the disease was available on the other bank. Only they seemed divested of the means of getting to that. The strong and sturdy physique they were proud of seemed meaningless and vague.

"Hello, boatman uncle! Where have you disappeared?" How panic-stricken and apprehensive the voice sounded! Had anyone in the surrounding area heard such an unnerving voice ever before? Could the river say when it had heard such a voice before? Could the sand on the river bed provide any information? What would the bushes on the bank reply? What would the boat, partly in water and partly on the sand, answer? Had the moon decided to hide its face for some time because it had never heard such a pathetic voice? Where did the sky suddenly disappear?

"Boatman uncle, please appear as soon as possible. Please save our world from being wrecked." The prayer reflected worry, disquiet and distress of a mother's heart. It was as if they were standing in front of a temple. When they were beseeching God to intervene, they suddenly discovered that there was no deity on the altar. God had suddenly disappeared. However, the crisis persisted; it showed no signs of dissipating. There was hardly any help coming from any quarter.

Soon, an uncontrollable rage spread through Nirakar's body. His mind sizzled. About five or six years ago, a huge meeting was organized in the field near the river bank. It was announced in the meeting that a bridge was going to be constructed over the river. The thousands of citizens who lived on this side of the river would find an easy access to the district headquarters. What great excitement spread through the people of this area! People wondered if the landscape of the area, long-neglected and prone to frequent floods, would really undergo a transformation as promised! Was this government so kind? Was the person who spoke on the mike so competent?

Not only four or five garlands, people were ready to leave a heap of garlands around his neck and at his feet. With their tears of gratefulness and gratitude, they were ready to wash his feet, which had hardly trod on dust and mud. A sense of utter delight had overtaken them. They wished, "Let the remaining years of the lives of the crowd gathered here be added to yours so that you live for a thousand years to render service to the poor. May all the problems that you encounter in life like the innumerable demands of the public, the frequent elections, and the personal debacles that beset your life and hinder your progress, be resolved. Let you remain imperishable and eternal in the minds of the people. Ah! How fortunate your parents are who bore a child like you. The entire earth and the sky reverberated with the cries of the crowd, "To hail with thee… to hail with thee". No other words emerged from their lips that day.

A marble plaque containing the name, designation and date was put up at the site. Two huge pillars emerged from the ground. Surprisingly, everything stopped soon thereafter. After a few days, obscene words replaced the words originally written on the plaque. After a few days, the plaque wasn't seen anymore. Many people who had joined the meeting that day preferred to pee on those pillars. The two pillars still exist. They carry the desire of turning themselves into Ahalya one day or the other. The iron rods at the top of the pillars have rusted and turned black. It appears as if two candles have been standing, carrying black wicks. Only, someone has to light them.

The dream of the people of the locality to have a bridge over the river remained unfulfilled. However, there was no end to the need for crossing the river. Do the necessities and demands of life postpone themselves, waiting for promises and hopes to be fulfilled? People still cross the river to reach the other bank. Items of every day use are still carried. Daughters leave for their in-laws' house. People with jobs attend their office. Litigants attend court dates; police officers reach to investigate cases of murder and bloodshed. The hindrance in the shape of the river is crossed many times to let the current of life flow unabated.

Everything continued as usual. The boat was still used as the means to cross the river. Patients were carried to the other side, just as Nirakar and Sumitra had brought their seriously ill child to be transported to the hospital on the other side. Unfortunately, the person whose services were badly needed on such occasions was absent. The boat was there; the oar was there; but the man whose skillful hands safely ferried people across the river was conspicuously missing.

"What shall we do now?" Sumitra's anxious query elicited no response.

Nirakar shouted again, "Boatman uncle. We've been waiting anxiously for you for a long time. It's urgent. Please be quick."

Abtar wasn't visible for the rescue act. His torch wasn't emitting any light. He spoke no words. Everything was silent, barring the sound of the flowing water.

"Let's go back home," proposed Sumitra. "I can't see any other way out."

The darkness and silence seemed so deep that even a sharp spade or an axe couldn't cut through them. Nirakar switched on the torch and felt the child's forehead once again with his palm. He felt as if all the heat on the earth had accumulated at that small area. The way the child was getting hiccups, even Charaka, the Father of Indian Medicine, would feel helpless and scared at the sight of the child.

Would the problem be solved if he went back home? Should he wait till the morning with the problem persisting with his child? The mere thought of the pain that his child was going through shattered his heart. What would he get if he waited till the morning? What comfort would the four walls of his house provide him? Would he helplessly watch his child leaving this world and going to the world beyond?

How could he allow his only child to leave this world so easily when he himself was alive? Why couldn't he ferry the child from this bank to the other? What was the point in possessing a robust body if it couldn't provide protection to his only child? Why should he live after all? Who would he live for?

Nirakar soon felt that his helplessness and powerlessness disappeared at this thought. He felt as if he had grown firm and stronger; as if his entire body expanded in form. He felt as if he would fly in the air and reach the other bank. He would pluck out the Gandhamardan Mountain just as Lord Hanuman had done. He would carry all the doctors on his shoulder and fly back.

Would something of this sort really happen?

Niirakar ordered his wife, "come."

"Where?" Sumitra asked, unable to decipher what he intended to say.

"Go to the boat." This was the order issuing from

a transformed Nirakar. "We shouldn't make any further delay. It's really getting late. We should do whatever is possible on our part quickly."

Nirakar had been transformed. Sumitra failed to comprehend whether what he was going to do should be interpreted as madness or some divine intervention through him.

"Why should we move forward? A frightened Sumitra asked.

She quipped, "Can't you see the boatman is absent? How are we supposed to cross the river? Are we going to swim or walk through water?"

"Don't talk nonsense." Nirakar behaved as if he was under the influence of some mysterious power. "Yes, I'll walk. You'll be there by my side. I'll hold the child aloft, over water. Then you'll see what the river is compelled to do. It'll give us way. There will hardly be any current or water where we step. We'll easily reach Gopapur. Today, history is going to be re-created. Today, Basudev is not alone. He'll be accompanied by Devaki. Let's go." Nirakar pulled Sumitra's hand towards him.

"Have you gone crazy?" Sumitra protested the moment she heard the bizarre plan. "Such things happen with Gods. Who are we? Should I support this whimsical decision of yours and jump into this deep, swiftly-flowing river? Leave my hand first. Let's go back home. I don't think we are going to get any help. Even the boatman is missing at a time when he is needed the most. And you are talking about God. Is there any guarantee that He will come to our rescue?"

Sumitra protested as much as she could but she found

herself getting dragged towards the flowing water. They soon reached the boat. Nirakar lifted the bicycle into it. He stretched his hand forward and said, "Come on... I say... clamber into the boat."

"No...no...please don't do anything foolish like this. In addition to protest there was an element of fervent appeal this time. Can you row the boat yourself? How would we cross such a wide river? I beseech you, please stop this madness..."

Two long bamboo poles and an oar lay in the boat. The boat was tethered to a peg on the bank. Nirakar released the rope and pushed the boat into water, till it reached the current. Soon he clambered into it. The moment he took the oar in his hands, he shuddered as though an electric current passed through his body. He had goosebumps all over.

Most significantly, he had never been that bold earlier. He had no idea what his actions would lead to—suicide or saving of a life. Irrespective of the results, he had accepted the challenge. He had enough physical energy to back that challenge. Besides, the determination to cross the river and anyhow reach the other bank spurred him on.

The boat left the bank and started moving. Sumitra, in a voice choked with emotion said, "Why are you trying to drown us? I tell you, stop here. Let's go back home. What our fate has in store will surely happen."

One end of the bamboo pole touched the sand under water. He had to exert pressure on that. Nirakar felt confident after repeating the exercise two or three times. All his energy and concentration were now centred on plying the boat safely.

Nirakar had, on many occasions in the past, seen the

boatman row the boat using the oar. Initially, when the boat left the bank it would go some distance against the current of the river. The bamboo pole would be used to push the boat against the current. The passengers riding the boat would feel the boat moving upstream for some time. Only then the boat would touch the destined point on the other bank. Nirakar had taken the oar in his hands once or twice, but only in the presence of the boatman. His aim, on those occasions, was to gather some experience. That had happened years ago. The present circumstances were completely different. He had to row the boat alone, without the guidance of the boatman, in the middle of the night. If he committed any mistake, disaster would surely befall.

Everything appeared dreadful and shrouded in mystery. The river looked like a black moving tongue. What if it felt disturbed and enraged by the rowing of the boat by inexperienced hands? What if it suddenly turned violent? How could someone put up with so much anxiety and disquiet? Sitting on a narrow plank that joined the prows, she had turned extremely frightful and panicky. Ominous thoughts clouded her mind. At times her thoughts would wander from the condition of the ill-child that she held close to her bosom. She was certain of only one thing—their end was drawing near.

The boat would shake violently at times, threatening to throw the mother and child off into water. She would close her eyes then. Her breathing would be constricted. Her blood circulation would stop. She would feel as if her heart was going to burst; her liver would be squeezed; her flesh and bones would dissolve.

How could the husband of hers, whom he had considered calm, composed and industrious for such a long time, turn out to be so reckless, insistent and crazy? His mindless rashness had driven her to such a state of uncontrolled, intense dread. She felt utterly helpless. She watched the figure moving on the boat. It would bend down at times; it would stand straight at others. Everything appeared so terrifying and eerie.

"Switch on the torch. Let me see how far we are from the other bank" sounded a voice gasping for breath. It hinted at the dipping energy, waning confidence and dwindling perseverance.

The torch light failed to locate anything. Its light spotted neither the bank they had left nor the other they intended to reach. Now they grew certain that they were floating in the middle of the river. Unintentionally, she focused the torch on Nirakar for some time.

His body glistened in perspiration. Nirakar, however, was unmindful of the slogging. He had started worrying because he felt his hands would tear off from his body. His muscles had started wearing out. His palms had turned red hot like ember. His palms would soon singe.

He now perceived that rowing a boat wasn't as easy as it seemed. His earlier experience with the boat had never revealed this lesson. In comparison to him, the boatman was weaker and more emaciated. He was balding too. Most of the hair on his moustache had turned grey. But he would row the boat as effortlessly as one would fan himself with a handfan.

Now he was certain he had inexperienced hands. Despite the best of his efforts, they couldn't row him to his destination. He was losing his energy and perseverance. His body was crumbling.

The problem had grown serious. Not only was the boat shaking violently but also it had lost its way. How come the other bank was out of sight when he had been rowing the boat for an eon? It was amply clear that the boat had entered the fathomless waters. What if they encountered whirlpools? Is it possible that ravenous crocodiles were lying in wait for them?

Suddenly, it seemed as if he had lost control over the oar. The boat now glided uncontrollably. They were floating downwards. Nirakar had no doubt now that he was losing the battle. What was written in their fate? Would the boat capsize? Would they float into the sea?

"What's the matter?" asked the immensely terrified Sumitra while dragging the child closer to her bosom. She shut her eyes tight in order not to witness the final accident.

"Put the child down. Let him sleep there. Stand up. Hold the other oar. The boat is floating downwards. It must be prevented from doing so." Nirakar's voice sounded different this time. There was a sense of urgency in it. This was, according to him, the best way to escape from the impending calamity.

Sumitra got up, tied the end of her saree around her waist and picked up the oar. She needed no instructions. She held the oar close to the prow on her end. After some time the boat headed towards the bank.

Sumitra didn't sit idly even for a second. Both of them couldn't see each other for certain; their manner of using the oars was incongruous no doubt; but both of them shared one wish--to reach the bank.

What a grand moment of relief it was! The boat touched the other bank. The drops of sweat running down from their wearied bodies and the tears of happiness spread a strange sensation. They soon discovered that they had not reached the spot where they should have but reached another, too far away downstream. They had successfully dealt with only one of their troubles.

Before commencing the next part of the journey, Nirakar felt the child's forehead and entire body with his palm. He was still running temperature. He was still getting hiccups. A strange excitement and emotion clutched Nirakar's heart. He was almost going to say, "You'll certainly get well. You'll regain your health and play in the courtyard of our house. I'll buy a football for you. You'll grow up and become a hefty young man. By that time, we two would have grown old. Your mother will narrate the incidents of today's night. You'll be amazed to hear how I behaved as if I was charmed by some magician. You'll look at yourself. You'll hardly believe the tale of the night and how we took you to Gopapur."

They heard the chirp of some bird as if still in sleep. A worried Nirakar asked if dawn was breaking. He was so lost in the rowing of the boat that he hadn't marked the passage of time. He then felt surprised that even after hours of struggle, the night was still not over.

They walked on a narrow footpath on the bank. It was not possible to ride the bicycle. They somehow continued progressing. Once they reached the spot where the boat should have usually touched the bank, they would easily find the way. Then they would enter a known territory.

They had disembarked at a spot about a kilometer away from the usual place. Soon they heard the sounds of vehicles that ran on the highway. They could see their lights too. The distant horizon appeared radiant because of the lights from the city.

He reached the residence of the doctor who had examined his child on the previous occasion. The gate was locked; the lights were off. Perhaps he was waking up a man from sleep after many years.

"Who is it?" A man's voice was heard after a moment of silence.

"Sir, please save my child."

The sound of door opening was heard; the lights were switched on.

Nirakar was certain the door would open. The lights would be switched on. A question enquiring what had happened to whom would emerge from inside. Despite lack of facilities crumpling their lives, a hope sustained him. That's why nothing —whether it was the river current, surrounding darkness, lack of help or inexperience could prevent persons like Nirakar from proceeding.

How could the short nap of a wearied Sumitra or a puncture in the bicycle tube deter him from fighting the battle?

❑

(Original Odia: *Gopapura*)

Story of A Moonlit Night

Tarun Kanti Mishra

Mother called out softly from the kitchen, "Children! Dinner is ready."

While serving food, mother doesn't call out so softly. She would rather shout, "Children, hurry up, food is ready", or "Stop jabbering, come here, quick!"

By children, she meant Banu uncle, my elder sister Pinky and me. The list included father if he was back home after closing the shop.

The evening-lamp lit at the sacred tulsi plant was still glowing and the moon was hanging from the branches of the wood-apple tree, when mother called us to dine.

We rarely dined so early. But that night, we had to go to bed early so that we could get up before sunrise. We had to vacate the house in the morning.

Mother called out once again, "Children, come and have your dinner."

We should have taken our seats, but I suddenly remembered one thing.

"Pinky Nani, I want to tell you something."

"What do you want to tell me, you fool?"

"Again ! Again you called me a fool?"

"Sorry, I'll not call you a fool again. Promise!"

"Ok, come with me."

I walked ahead, with Pinky Nani following me. We cleaned five plantain leaves. We sat on the verandah near the kitchen. The leaves were meant for Banu uncle, Pinky Nani and me. And of course, two more for parents.

We usually didn't eat food on plantain leaves but it was different tonight. All our utensils had been packed. All the furniture, books and clothes had been packed too. We just had to pass the night.

Banu uncle fetched water for all of us in plastic glasses. We sat waiting for mother.

Mother called out to father, "You hear me? Do you want to eat now?"

Father, who was lying on a mat in the other room, responded, "I'm not hungry."

Father's reply sounded strange to me. He was at home all the day; he hadn't gone to the shop. He packed our belongings throughout the day. At lunchtime he had said he wasn't interested to eat anything. And now he said he was not hungry.

I knew why he was sad.

Mother told us, "We just have rice and potatoes; you have to manage with that."

Pinky *Nani* had a habit to whine. She would grumble, "I won't eat this...I won't eat that." If there were *parathas*, she would demand *purees*; if *purees* were served, she would ask for *dhoklas*. She would eat mango chutney and carp that it was excessively sweet; and, on eating mango pickles, she would complain it was too sour.

But these days, she seemed to have changed. She would quietly eat whatever mother would give. She would also praise mother for her cooking.

Raising her head a little from the leaf plate, Pinky Nani announced, "Mother, the potato curry tastes great!"

Mother came near us and asked, "Do you want a little more?"

Pinky *Nani* replied, "No, Mommy, I am fine. And don't give him any more. He has also enough on his plate."

Had it been another day, Pinky *Nani* would have leaped and bawled, "Yeah...yeah... give me more." She would have wanted more of chicken, more of ice cream, more of *kheer,* more of everything. And she'd leave them almost untouched.

She doesn't behave that way anymore. These days, not too many items are cooked at home. Pandav, our cook, has left. Now mother cooks. She does every chore in the house: cooking, washing, cleaning, everything.

"Why did you throw away the cake, half-eaten?" Pinky *Nani* had scolded me on my birthday, a few days back.

My birthday, last year, was celebrated at Hotel Orchid. About two hundred guests were invited. They brought me many gifts and sang, "Happy birthday to Sipun!"

This year, my birthday was celebrated at home. None other than my uncles and aunties joined. Father presented me a T-shirt. I didn't like it much.

"Why did you throw away the cake, half-eaten?"

When Pinky Nani badgered me with that question I said, "I didn't like the taste of that cake. It smelt rotten."

She was startled as if I had spoken something filthy. She stole a look at our parents. They were busy collecting the used plates; they hadn't heard anything.

Pinky Nani would always caution me. "Don't waste food, don't lose your pen, don't insist on buying new shoes, don't ever ask for money to buy ice-creams, and don't use the fan for long hours ..."

"How can I do without the fan? We don't have the air conditioner any more. Can I do my learning without a fan?"

Pinky *Nani* would try to explain, father has little money now.

"If he is short on money, he should sell more and more things in his shop."

"You don't understand. He is making losses."

"Loss? What do you mean by loss?"

I understood what loss meant. Loss meant 'No Money'. We had now become poor.

Since the day I was promoted to Standard Four, that is, over the last one year, things had gone topsy-turvy. No more do we visit Bangalore, Puri, not even Nandankanan, during the holidays. Our car has been sold off. Our refrigerator that had gone out of order couldn't be replaced. And I have already told you about my last birthday, haven't I?

Four months back, when our cook Pandav was asked to leave, he broke down. Mother also had tears in her eyes.

Father said, "I'm sorry, Pandav. Please go back to your home. We can't manage anymore."

Pandav said, "No, uncle, don't ask me to leave. I'll pull through somehow."

Father said, "Pandav, do try to understand. Your wages are due for months on end. I haven't been able to pay. You know how much money I earn these days and how much I need to manage the household. I can't take any extra burden."

Pandav wiped off tears from his eyes. He touched the feet of my parents. He picked up his iron trunk and went out. The trunk contained, among others, father's used clothes, some of mother's worn-out sarees and one of my old toys.

Had he taken away my old toy some other day, I would have banged my head and rolled on the ground. I don't know what happened to me that day; I remained quiet.

Mother silently watched Pandav walking away with his head bent down. She wiped her tears. Not because she had now more household work to do but because she loved him - like her son...I mean...like me.

Pinky *Nani* repeated, "Mommy, potato tastes delicious. No, no! I don't want any more please. Sipun also doesn't need any more."

Pinky *Nani* and I have a secret sign language which no one can follow. She warned me not to ask for more, as there was very little left for others.

I came out to the courtyard to wash my hands. Then I looked up and saw the moon. It was gorgeous. I always believed the moon that visited our courtyard was our own. It belonged to us. It was different from the moon we saw on the sea-beach at Puri or the moon that we saw at the park, or at the railway station.

My heart writhed in pain when I remembered that we'd have to bid goodbye to this courtyard and this moon of ours. We'd never ever return to this house.

This house was ours. My grandfather had built it even before Banu uncle was born. Father had added a few more rooms, a garden and a balcony. It always appeared enchanting.

A few days ago, mother told us that we had to leave this house.

"Why?" I had asked.

"Why?" Pinky *Nani* had asked.

"This house has been sold off."

"Why, why?"

Mother's eyes welled up. She tried hard to snatch a smile. And she said, "The new house we're shifting to has a park near it. It is close to your school, also to father's shop."

Soon we learnt everything. That new house was a small apartment. It had only one bathroom. No courtyard, no garden.

That night father didn't eat anything, nor did mother. The two leaf plates lay abandoned on the verandah. The moon shone on the courtyard in its solitary silence.

I observed father, who was moving like a shadow, from room to room, as if searching for some lost object. He'd switch on the lights and his gaze would wander about the room, and then he'd switch the lights off.

What was there to look for? All rooms had been emptied. All articles had been neatly packed and stored in the two rooms at the front. The truck was expected to arrive in the morning. We had to get ready quickly.

Mother was also following father from room to room. They moved through the drawing room, the study, the bedrooms...

Father stood silently in front of their bed room. As if he was waiting for someone.

Mother, who was following him, said, "Do you remember, the day after our marriage ceremony... you entered this room and found me here alone and then ... Do you remember ?"

Mother tried to flash her sweet smile, the one I always longed to see. But she failed. Two big drops of tear rolled down her cheeks. She moved away from there, and stood in front of the *puja* room.

This corner room was grandfather's favorite haunt. In the morning, he'd be found here lost in meditation. In the evening, he would recite *shloka*s from the scriptures. He had turned vegetarian after the death of grandmother. He possessed only a pair of dhotis and a couple of shawls.

My grandfather was very rich. No, actually my grandmother was rich. She had plenty of money and jewellery. Our house is built on her ancestral land.

After grandmother's death, grandfather lost all his zest for life and turned an ascetic. He'd spend half of his time in the garden and the other half in this *puja* room.

My mother says, grandfather was very generous. He'd give away money to poor and destitute secretly; my parents wouldn't have an inkling of what he was doing.

My grandfather would often tell my mother, "Daughter, don't ever forget to pay your obeisance to these Gods. Your fortune lies here only, below the throne of these Gods".

Mother would regularly offer her prayers to the gods; she'd burn incense sticks and light *diya*s at their altar.

My father would at times tell mother, "It's good that Dad is giving away money to the poor and needy; but why this hush-hush? I never had any objection to his acts of charity."

The gist of what mother would say is this: One doesn't earn piety if he makes a show of his generosity.

The day father lost the case in the Court, he came back home disheartened and distressed. Glaring at mother, who was then squatting in the *puja* room and offering her prayers, he hissed:

"So these are your Gods ! These are your benevolent Masters!"

Quietly, mother looked at father. In her eyes, there was a silent prayer, an ardent invocation.

Our situation had worsened after losing that case. The car and all ornaments of mother had to be sold.

"I couldn't save anything for Pinky's marriage," sobbed mother one night.

Father had changed a lot. His sunny smile had disappeared. His eyes were sinking.

Mother was standing silently near the *puja* room. The lonely moon was glancing down from above the courtyard. Father approached her with gentle steps.

He said, "Would you like to pack the idols now ? You may not get enough time in the morning."

Mother had planned to collect the idols of Gods into a cardboard box in the morning, after taking bath and offering prayers.

Now she thought for a moment and said, "I think I should do the packing tonight. In the morning, I guess, I might have… some difficulty… "

Father said, "In that case, finish up everything now."

Father went to the front room, which was earlier our drawing-room. He had some papers lying in that room which he wanted to sort out.

He saw me in the dark verandah. He said, "Sipun, go to sleep. Ask Pinky to go to bed, too. It's very hot; turn the fan on."

Mother entered the *puja* room. She sat near the idol of Lord Madhusudan, as if she were His little daughter. She sat there, crestfallen. She wiped her tears in the corner of her *saree*.

Mother was wearing a gorgeous and expensive *saree*. It was very old and ripped at places. She decided to use it for one last time before discarding it forever.

I didn't know the reason why, but I felt like weeping. Mother had put on such a lovely *saree*; her face looked so beautiful in the blue light of the *puja* room; Lord Madhusudan's statue glittered on the throne, but I felt like weeping.

Father had once sneered at her, "Go on worshipping these idols, day in and day out. Now what had Dad told you? ' Don't forget to pray these gods every day, your fate lies at the foot of their throne'!"

I looked at the courtyard. The moon had moved far away to that part of the sky beyond the Silk-cotton tree from where it wasn't clearly visible. Evening air, now still and stifled, was languishing in the dark. Perched in the hollow of a tree, an owl was sobbing intermittently, in sad nostalgia.

Mother was sitting all alone in the *puja* room. She was collecting the idols of Lord Madhusudan and all other Gods in a cardboard box. Grandfather had been using a huge iron chest as the altar. Spreading a silk cloth over it, he had placed all the idols and pictures of Gods. Mother continued with that practice after grandfather's death.

The iron chest was gigantic and cumbersome. Father had suggested, "No need to open it. We'll carry it to the new place just as it is."

Mother started wiping the dust off the iron chest carefully. After all, this was our grandfather's vault, you see!

Suddenly, a clanging noise came from the kitchen. Nobody heard the sound except me.

I ran to the kitchen.

I found Pinky *Nani* standing alone in the kitchen, shuddering in dread.

On the floor lay a glass bowl, smashed into pieces. In this bowl mother had saved some curd, to be taken next morning to mark our auspicious journey.

Now the bowl was shattered into pieces. Shreds of glass lay scattered on the floor.

Pinky *Nani* thought I'd instantaneously rush to our parents and report against her. In dread of that, she kept looking at me pathetically, without uttering a word.

I reached near her.

Immediately, she burst into tears and said...

No, there was no need for her to tell me anything; I saw everything clearly. Thinking that mother must have grown tired, slogging throughout the day, she had washed the woks and bowls, wiped the gas stove clean and cleansed the basin. It was the same Pinky *Nani* who wouldn't even wash her cup after drinking water from it.

When she was placing the woks and bowls on the shelf after cleaning them, the glass bowl containing curd had dropped.

The pieces of glass lay here and there. The curd lay scattered all over. Then I noticed a drop of blood.

"You hurt yourself!"

I bent down to her feet. "Let me see!"

Not much blood had oozed, just a few drops.

"Wait a little, *Nani*. Let me apply some ointment. I won't tell anyone anything."

Right then, mother's voice was heard from the *puja* room.

"Do you hear me?" She called out to father.

She called out as if she was alarmed; her second call had a tremor of surprise; and her last call echoed the helplessness of one who was lost in the woods.

We rushed to the *puja* room - father, I and Pinky *Nani*.

Mother was sitting beside the iron chest, in a trance. As if a magician had turned her into stone.

The iron chest was lying open.

The story was like this. After she had placed the idols and pictures of deities in a cardboard box, she fixed her gaze at the iron chest of grandfather. She took a towel and wiped it clean. Then she opened its lid.

She found some old *sarees*; all those once belonged to our grandmother. Underneath lay one of her pictures. A smiling grandmother looked enigmatically from the corners of her eyes. She looked as if she knew some great secrets she wouldn't reveal, because grandfather had forbidden her.

After she had picked up the picture, mother saw something that dazed her.

Yes, she was completely stunned. When I reached there, she was sitting there with her eyes shut.

And my bemused father, like a machine, was picking out one thing after another from the big iron chest. As if he was acting under a spell.

From that big heavy iron chest, father was taking out gold coins, precious jewels of different colors - perhaps those were all diamonds, pearls, sapphires, rubies. Under the blue light of the *puja* room, gemstones glittered.

Had it been some other day, Pinky *Nani* would have flung herself on those jewellery and picked up one, exclaiming, "This one is mine".

But she didn't do any such thing. She stood silently and watched the proceedings as one would watch a magic show, while father picked out pieces of jewellery.

I inched closer to her and whispered, *"Nani!"*

"Hmm…" "Let's go. I'll apply some ointment to your wound. Otherwise, it would worsen by tomorrow. It would hurt you even more." Both of us came out to the courtyard, hand in hand.

The moon had by then disappeared from our courtyard. Let it be. I will surely meet him tomorrow - maybe in this courtyard, maybe in some other corner of the world.

❑

(Original Odia: *Jahna Ratira Galpa*)

The Decision

Gourahari Das

Sonu never let go an opportunity to display his talent. If he found a ready audience, he would start singing the songs he had learnt by heart or drawing the artwork he had mastered. However, his stock of songs had finished by the time he travelled from Bhubaneswar to Cuttack. He had to travel till Bhadrak. So he said, "Mommy, it would have been better if we had carried all my books".

Grandmother Sulochana burst out to a laugh. The other co-passengers were amused to hear his childish babbles. Sonu's mother said, "It's okay for the time being. Give a little rest to your songs. Look, how beautiful the trees and paddy fields look!"

"Should I draw pictures?"

Nilima smiled. Sonu's drawing notebook was in the bag placed on the baggage carrier. She said, "You can draw pictures only when we reach our village. Your notebook and pencil are there in the bag on the luggage carrier. Relax. Just have a look outside and see things."

Sonu appeared dispirited.

The elderly gentleman sitting on the seat nearby called him near him and said, "Come here...boy...come. What's your name?"

Sonu was in dire need of this kind of attention. He fervently wished that all the passengers sitting in the compartment should either listen to his stories and songs or talk to him. He felt inspired and proudly said, "I'm Seemanta Mohapatra but you can call me Sonu".

The gentleman caressed his hair. As he had a haircut a couple of days back, his head looked stubby like a newly sprouting pasture. Sulochana was on her way to her in-laws' village after a long time accompanied by elder son Sidharth, daughter-in-law Nilima and grandson Sonu. She had left the village about twenty years back. When Sidhu's father was alive, she visited it at times. But after his death, she had failed to maintain any relationship with it. Her brother-in-law Banamali and his children enjoyed whatever the fields of their share produced. Earlier, they would send some rice or a few coconuts when they willed but for the last two years, they had stopped sending even those. When Sidhu's father was alive Sulochana would frequently remind him, "Why are you leaving the whole of the property of your father and fore-fathers in the hands of thieves and robbers? Don't you realize that our children are in difficulties here? If you sell the landed property of your share and bring them the sale proceeds, they can at least use the amount to construct a house."

Sidhu's father would hear everything and nod his head. He would sit in a solemn posture as if he had taken a final decision. He would leave for village one fine day. He would stay there for a day or two and return, just as empty handed as he had gone. Sulochana would ask him, "What decision have you taken regarding disposal of the ancestral property?"

While unpacking the sack of its contents like a few coconuts, a few *oous*, some spinach, a few brinjals and a piece of pumpkin, Sidhu's father would say, "I've already conveyed my message to them. Whatever our children decide would be carried out. For the time being, the paddy remains to be cultivated. We'll think of selling it towards the month of *Magha*." Twenty *Maghas* had gone by but the landed property at Patapur couldn't be disposed of. Sidhu's father departed for his heavenly abode in the meantime. Sulochana would often think, "Many good customers had approached them with money. Raghav Parida had gone to extent of saying that even after paying all the money towards the land, he would send some paddy for the worship of goddess Lakshmi on *Manabasa Gurubar* and some rice every year for their consumption at Bhubaneswar. Sadly, Sidhu's father could never make up his mind."

Sulochana would blame her younger sister-in-law for all the troubles. The lady, who most of the time remained mum, was one not to trifle with. She would have addressed Sidharth's father as 'elder brother' affectionately. She would have lovingly served a bowlful of *pakhala* with a few pieces of hilsa fish or a few pieces of *paratha*s with a little cheese and a bowl of *kheer*. With her pretentious behavior, she would have bowled over the elder brother-in-law, who in turn would have forgotten everything about the disposal of ancestral property. Just the way that pretentious Pratima behaved, so did her husband. He knew pretty well that his brother could be won over with a few kilos of vegetables and a kilo of prawn.

Every member of Sulochana's family was well-versed with the accusations she made. Sidhu's father would say, "Even renowned poets have opined, women and jealousy are two sides of the same coin. Are you expected to be different?"

Sidharth would say, "If you know so many things, why don't you go with father to the village? You can keep a watch on the movements of father then."

Sulochana would sneer and say, "Do I care what he does? I've to take care of Sonu. Buna has sent a message that she'll arrive soon from Rourkella. Besides, the dark fortnight of *Ashwin* when the ritual *shradh* is offered to the dead ancestors falls two days after the full moon day. Who has the time or leisure to go to that inaccessible village which even the Pandavas didn't visit? The landed property belongs to his forefathers; let him go there and dispense with it the way he likes."

The reasons that Sulochana placed to justify her busy schedule would amuse everybody. They would burst into a laugh. Sulochana would leave for the kitchen, with an anger-ridden face.

Ajay Sutar had arranged a taxi for their journey from Bhadrak to Patapur. They got down at the Charampa station and took the taxi. Sulochana had been insisting on visiting Patapur for about a month. But the Gadi-Patapur road was under repair. Two canals ran near Sashubhuasuni and Haldia; in the absence of bridges, people had to change into towels to cross those. The road work was completed about fifteen days back and the road was opened for vehicular traffic. Sulochana found that the loquacious Sonu had become tired and was about to fall asleep. She moved closer to the window of the car and let Sonu sleep in her lap. She remembered God and beseeched Him to protect her children under the cover of His conch and discus.

Five years had elapsed since the death of Sidhu's father. Last *Baisakh*, Sidhu went to Prayag, the confluence of the Ganga, the Yamuna and the Saraswati and consigned the bones into water. From Allahabad he went to Gaya and from there to Benaras to have a *darshan* of Lord Kashiviswanath. After returning to Jajpur, he offered *shradh* once again. He immediately left for Puri to have a *darshan* of Lord Jagannath. Sulochana looked at her son's face; there was hardly any difference between his nature and that of his father. He would hardly blame others for the troubles he faced; he would never deter from carrying out his responsibilities. He had a fervent wish—to construct a house at Bhubaneswar. But every pie that he earned went to meet the daily expenses of the family. If the landed property was sold, she would give him seventy-five percent of what they got so that he could fulfill his dream.

Sulochana looked outside through the window of the taxi. She hadn't visited her in-law's place for a long time. The sights on both sides of the road from Bhadrak to Gadi had transformed significantly. Many residential dwellings had come up in the places where barren pastures spread once. If this continued, there would hardly be any open space left between Bhadrak and Chandabali.

Sidharth was sitting on the front seat. He was delighted to think that the problems that had persisted for a long time were going to be resolved. Since his father bore an emotional attachment with the ancestral property, he was finding it difficult to sell. He read the feelings of his mother quite well. She was born and brought up in Cuttack, and consequently bore absolutely no fascination for this swampy village. She would always make fun of father, when he was alive, saying, "If you ever want to torture a bride, see that she gets married in Patapur. She would lose all her energy blowing into the chullah during the rainy season, and carrying water home during the summer season."

Sidhu's father would devise different plans on such occasions to silence her. He would say, "You visit the village once in a blue moon like a tourist. Why are you so worried about how the brides suffer there? Won't those who live in the village take care of themselves?"

Sidharth informed, "Mother, listen to me carefully. I've asked three prospective customers to come at three different times. You can have a discussion with each one of them but keep the final decision reserved. We may have to stay for an additional day but we must return with some advance money from the one who makes the best offer. Besides, we have to hand over the possession of the land to the buyer. Have you seen all our landed property?"

"Do you think this is a city? There the neighbors even can't tell who the next plot of land belongs to. But here, things are different. If you ask one which pieces of land belong to the Mohapatra family, the entire village will come up with answers. Besides, your uncle is also there to guide you. It is he who has been cultivating the land of our share and keeping the entire produce."

Sidharth nodded.

By the time they reached the Ghanteswar market, it was already four thirty in the afternoon. Sidharth's uncle Banamali was waiting at the market. Sidharth got off the taxi and said 'namaskar' to his uncle. Nilima drew the veil over her head and paid her respect to her uncle-in-law. Banamali came to his sister-in-law Sulochana and paid his respects. He took Sonu out and carried him. He had already placed orders with Laxmidhar Sahu, a sweetmeat seller in the market, to get some cheesecake and *rasogollas* ready. Fresh *bada*s were being fried. Each of them gobbled up three or four *badas* and drank water from the bottles they had carried with them. They had tea too. Banamali bought some specially ordered betel cones from a nearby shop and handed them over to Sulochana. Sidharth and Nilima dropped a few cloves into their mouths. Sonu demanded some mango-flavoured chocolates.

Banamali sat on the front seat of the same taxi. Sidharth accommodated himself on the back seat. Cars very rarely appear on the Ghanteswar-Patapur road. Whenever an acquaintance looked at Banamali with inquisitive eyes, he would smile and say, "My sister-in-law has come. We are going home." Those people would show their respect to Sulochana. They would discuss among themselves, "Don't you know? She is Mana Mohapatra's wife. She now stays with her children in the state capital."

Sulochana sat on the rear seat swelling with the pride of a landlady. She had her family with her. She was well acquainted with the surroundings. She would point out to Nilima enthusiastically, "This is the pandal where the Durga idol is worshipped; this is Ghanteswar High School; both Sidhu and Bunu received their early education here; this is the village Mahadev temple; this one is the village pond. The day fish is caught from this pond, all the villagers crowd here for their share. This one is Arjun Babaji's pond. Baniapada is on the other side of it. And the river that is visible from here is called…"

"Mantei," interjected Sonu.

All of them burst into laughter with this display of his knowledge of the landscape.

Banamali picked Sonu and placed him on his lap. He said, "Look how the village soil attracts its own people. Despite being only five years of age, he remembers the name of the river flowing by his village."

The Chandrasekhar Mahadev temple of Patapur stood in front of them.

Banamali's grand-daughter was two years elder to Sonu. She held Sonu by his hand and took him around the village. Sonu, clad in colourful dresses, was an attraction for the half-clad children of the village. They formed groups and accompanied him. Mili showed him the trees of the village. "This is the babul tree. If you step on its thorn, it pains a lot. This tree gives tamarind that is sour to taste. This tree yields yellow oleander flowers and this tree produces carambola fruits. That pond is called 'Tubi Gadia' and it has a variety of fish such as climbing perch fish, scorpion fish and sheat fish.

Sonu observed everything minutely, surprise writ large on his face. Banamali sat on the front verandah. He was found informing Sidharth, "Tender has been floated three times but the road from Nua Pokhari to the village can't be black-topped. The village has electricity connection no doubt but most of the time the supply is disrupted. Thieves are running away with supply wires. Nobody in the village is concerned for a common cause. One has to run to Ghanteswar bazzar just for a pill in case of fever. In such a situation, how can I leave the village and go somewhere. The Ghanteswar-Gadi road opened a few days ago bringing some relief, otherwise what immense trouble one had to face to travel! Can't you convey our grievances to someone who can solve those?

Sidharth wasn't at all interested in what Banamali was saying. He was as if saying, "If you have so many problems to encounter in the village, why don't you shift to Ghanteswar. Your son is making a handsome income from his grocery shop. Where is the trouble?" Banamali's words entered from one side of his ear and escaped through the other. He was only interested in the money that Sridhar Mohanty was going to bring him. He would take the money and leave the village, that's all.

It was already eight in the morning. They had to leave soon otherwise the fierce sun of *Ashwin* would scorch them.

Sidharth got up and went inside. What he saw there made him extremely surprised. Nilima was sitting on an ancient bedstead and the daughter-in-law of the village barber was anointing her feet with lac-dye. Sitting nearby his mother was found telling, "Daughter…you people get an annual fee for anointing our feet with lac-dye. See that my daughter-in-law had a nice coat of lac-dye around her feet. You know…Nilima, when I entered the family as a bride, Rama's mother-in-law would arrive on all festive occasions to anoint my feet."

The courtyard of Mohapatra family was circular in shape. The kitchen was in the middle, with rooms in front. The kitchen divided the huge courtyard into two. Whereas the men of the family conducted their business from the courtyard towards the front side of the house, the women conducted their worldly affairs from the courtyard on the back side. Sulochana was found reminiscing events of the past: this was where *badis* were left to dry in the sun; during festive occasions vegetables were cut. This was where she had learnt lessons in managing worldly affairs from her mother-in-law while watching stars twinkle in the evening sky. This was where her elder son played. Even this was the place where he had learnt to walk.

Pratima was busy packing things. She said, "Sister, this is the Lilabati variety of rice produced in the twelve-acre patch of land of yours. Mother-in-law would always praise you for cooking this rice well. I was always accused of over-cooking it. These are coconuts from our backyard. Had anyone else of the village planted coconut trees before elder brother did? This is the first coconut tree planted by elder brother. This is the *Oou* fruit. Since you had a special liking for it, your father had brought a sapling from Cuttack to be planted in our backyard. I have also packed some spinach and arum. The fried prawns are there in that box. Yesterday was Thursday; you didn't even touch the non-veg food.

She called out to her granddaughter and said, "Mili, where is the bunch of plantain?"

Banamali ran and returned with the bunch of plantain. He smiled and said, "Sister-in-law, this is the *bantala* variety that you always preferred. I always tell others, the delicious way you can fry pieces of plantain with cumin seeds and chilly powder, no other lady of our village can do that. How heavenly it tastes!"

Drops of perspiration ran down Banamali's body. He was wiping his fair-face with a towel at times.

Sidharth said, "What's the need of packing so many of these?"

Banamali replied, "Son, we don't have a fridge here;

so, we can't keep these preserved for a long time. What's the problem with you? Sister-in-law likes to eat this plantain fried. The *dahikadi* and plantain fry that she prepares lend a different taste to the food."

Pratima was found saying, "Sister, look… this is *sunsunia sag*; this is *kalama sag*; and this is *leutia sag*. Besides, I have packed a palmful of *badi*. I couldn't get more of these for you. Don't forget to tell me how these tasted. I've packed some ghee in this Horlicks bottle."

Banamali said, "I've packed two packets of rice of the Lilabati variety and another two packets of rice of the Patini variety in the dickey of the car. You must all be eating fine rice. I'll send money in lieu of rest of the rice of your share."

At that time Raju, Banamali's son, arrived with something in a bucket. He kept the bucket down and said, "I got only four of these sheat fish."

The live sheat fish were shaking their tails. Drops of water fell on Sidharth's face. He bore a special fascination for sheat fish in his childhood. His mother put some dried mango pieces to add a sour taste to the soup. His father believed that sheat fish formed blood in the body. He had not even seen live sheat fish for a very long time. The visions of childhood flashed before his eyes once again."

Raju informed, "Sridhar Mohanty is sitting on the front verandah."

Nilima had her feet anointed with lac-dye by then. Sidharth found her munching a betel cone. The stains from the betel cone had made her lips red. He said, "Bah! You seem to be enjoying your life a lot here as a daughter-in-law."

Nilima smiled. Her smile brightened up the dark room.

Sridhar handed over a newspaper wrapped packet into Sulochana's hand. He said, "Sister-in-law, I'll visit you after the Dussehra and pay the rest of the money. You can visit the village at your convenience some day later for the registration formalities."

Sulochana marked Banamali's face wilting the moment he heard the words 'registration'.

They were ready to leave. Banamali, Pratima, Raju, Mili and Sridhar Mohanty stood near the car. Sidharth marked, neither Sulochana nor Sonu had come out.

He went inside and hollered, "Mother!"

Sulochana was found standing near an old bedstead. She told, "You know Sidhu, when I came here for the first time as a bride, I sat on this bedstead. Fifty years have passed but nothing has happened to it."

Sidharth didn't utter a word. He went out in search of Sonu. After he went out, Sulochana looked here and there once, and sat on the bedstead. An old photo of her husband was hanging on the wall. She felt as if he had emerged from the photo and was sitting by her. A lamp burnt in one corner of the house.

Sulochana shut her eyes.

Memory of the last fifty years lay embedded on the walls of the house. Her elder son was born here. She had started her life as a bride here. She had learnt her life's lessons here. This was where she had indulged in arguments, tiffs and quarrels with her husband; this was where she had bathed under her husband's love and affection. Wherever she looked, she found the incidents associated with her past life painted with bright, bold strokes.

Sulochana wiped the tear that had welled up in her eyes and looked up at the roof of that ancestral house. The wooden inner roof had soot and spider webs stuck to it. The walls were laced with vermillion and collyrium marks over the years. The room smelled musty. However, to Sulochana the entire room looked wonderful. It was as if someone had dabbed the walls with camphor and sandalwood paste.

Multiple questions, raising their heads, made her restless. Was she doing anything wrong by selling the portion that belonged to her?

She remembered, every time she would pester her husband to sell the property, he would say, "This time I'll take a final decision." But every time he would return without having made up his mind. When asked about his indecision, he would only reply, "Let the children take a decision."

Her children had taken the decision to sell their share of the property now. How could Sulochana be faulted with? Then it surfaced in her mind, had she not incited her children by talking ill of her sister-in-law and her husband? Had Banamali lived a grand life here? It's true that he had not been able to send their portion of the produce regularly to them, but he hadn't gobbled up everything himself. The poor man was the patriarch of a large family; they had consumed everything.

She caressed the old wooden bedstead.

The lifeless wooden bedstead created a hum like that of a lute-string, creating a flutter in each memory cell.

Sidhu was calling out to her, "Mother…just come out and see this boy."

Sulochana wiped her eyes and emerged from the room. Banamali had arranged new clothes for all. While removing the printed paper from a corner of her saree, she asked, "What happened?"

Sidharth pointed at Sonu and said, "Look at him".

Sulochana looked at the boy and found *guguchia* fruits and dew drops stuck to his pants. Perhaps he was sitting on the ground. Mud had stuck to his heels and thighs. He had his drawing notebook in his hand.

"What's that?"

Sulochana found that her grandson had drawn a picture with Mantei River in the background. He had also drawn a few trees, birds and the sky. Below the picture, he had written, in his crooked handwriting, "Patapur—Our Village".

Sulochana felt flabbergasted. She dragged Sonu to her lap. While removing the *guguchia* fruits from his pants she told Sidhu, "Go and sit in the car. I'll come back in a minute."

She summoned Sridhar near her and said, "Sridhar, will you please listen to me?"

Sridhar went near her.

Sulochana took out the bundle of notes from the corner of her saree and returned it to him.

Taken by surprise by this unexpected move, Sridhar asked, "What is this, sister-in-law?"

Sulochana replied, "I pondered over the whole thing

for a very long time, Sridhar. Who am I to take a decision regarding the ancestral property of Mohapatra family? You just saw the picture drawn by one who is supposed to take the decision. The property has existed like this for a long time; let it be like this. I always blamed Sidhu's father as he was always indecisive about disposing it off. I had failed to comprehend earlier that by not taking a decision he had in fact taken the best decision."

Sridhar hardly knew how to respond.

❏

(Original Odia: *Nispati*)

Glossary

Anna: A former monetary unit equal to one-sixteenth of a rupee.

Ashwin: Seventh month of the Hindu calendar.

Bada: Odia deep fried balls made using black gram, onion, green chilli, semolina, salt etc.

Badi: Sundried lentil dumplings, popular in Odisha.

Baisakh: Month of Hindu calendar corresponding to April, May and June.

Baul: Mimusops elengi. Also known as Spanish cherry.

Bhadrab: Sixth month of the Hindu calendar.

Bhajan: Songs sung by the devotees in praise of the lord.

Bhog: Food offered to a deity.

Biri: A cheap form of cigarette made from cut tobacco rolled in a leaf.

Chhatank: An old Indian measure equivalent to sixty grams.

Dahikadi: A thick, yellowish yogurt or curd based curry.

Dalma: An authentic recipe of Odisha made using Arhar dal, vegetables etc.

Darshan:	The visit of a devotee to the lord.
Dhokla:	A Gujarati light and delicious snack made using gram flour, salt, water, lemon juice etc.
Diya:	A lighted earthen lamp.
Dolapurnima:	A day before Holi, a Hindu festival.
Gauni:	An age old Odia measuring tool.
Guguchia:	A weed.
Jhulanjatra:	A festival for the followers of Lord Krishna celebrated in the monsoon month of Shravan.
Kaliyug:	In Hinduism, the last of the four stages the world goes through as a part of the cycle of yugas.
Kheer:	Sweet rice pudding.
Kirtan:	Narrating, reciting, or telling spiritual or religious ideas.
Kosh:	A distance of 0.2 km.
Madhumalti:	Combretum Indicum. Also known as the Chinese honeysuckle.
Magha:	Tenth month of the Hindu calendar.
Magha Purnami:	The full moon day in the tenth month of the Hindu calendar.
Mahant:	Heads of Monasteries.
Manabasa Gurubara:	The Thursdays of the ninth month of Hindu calendar. Goddess Lakshmi is worshipped on this day.
Math:	A monastery.
Namaskar:	Derived from the Sanskrit 'Namas' meaning salutation or greetings.

Nauti:	Standard measure for corn used in the past.
Nani:	An address to an elder sister.
Nolia:	Traditional fishermen living on the sea-shore.
Pakhala:	Indian food consisting of cooked rice washed or a little fermented in water.
Paratha:	A flatbread.
Phalguna:	Eleventh month of the Hindu calendar.
Puja:	The act of worshipping the deity.
Purana:	Hindu religious text part of the Vedas.
Ramnavami:	Hindu festival that celebrates the birthday of Lord Rama.
Rasaleela:	Dance of Cosmic Consciousness with individualized consciousness.
Rasogolla:	Indian syrupy dessert made from ball shaped dumplings of cheese.
Sahada:	Streblus asper; also known as Siamese rough bush.
Sankirtan:	Same as Kirtan.
Saree:	Garment consisting of a length of cotton or silk draped around the body by women in India.
Satyayug:	The first of the four yugas; the 'Yuga of Truth'.
Shloka:	A couplet of Sanskrit verse.
Shradh:	A form of worship: A Vedic ritual performed to pay homage to ancestors.
Siuli:	*Nyctanthes abor-tristis;* night flowering jasmine.
Tola:	Equivalent to ten grams of gold.
Tribhanga:	A standing body position used in traditional Indian art and Indian Classical dance forms.

Writers' Profile

Fakir Mohan Senapati (1843-1918): Regarded as the father of Odia Nationalism and Modern Odia literature. He was a novelist, short story writer, poet, philosopher and social reformer—all blended into one. His Odia story *Rebati* (1898) is recognized as the first Odia short story. His novels *Chha Mana Atha Guntha, Mamu, Prayaschita* and *Lachhama* present the realities of social life in its multiple dimensions. In his stories he dealt with the common man and his problems. Odia nationalism was a dominant theme in most of his works.

Gopinath Mohanty (1914-1991): Recipient of many significant awards like the first Central Sahitya Akademi award ever given to a literary work, The Jnanpith Award, The Soviet Land Nehru Award and the Padma Bhusan award in recognition of his distinguished contribution to literature he was the 'most important Indian novelist in the second half of the twentieth century'. He has written twenty-four novels, ten collections of short stories, three plays, two biographies, two volumes of critical essays, and five books on the language of the Kondhs, Gadaba and Saora tribes. Among his significant contributions important are *Mana Gahirara Chasa, Dadi Budha, Paraja, Amrutara Santana*. In his writings he deals with the life of the tribal community.

Surendra Mohanty (1922-1990): Recipient of the Central Sahitya Akademi award, Odisha Sahitya Akademi award and Sarala award for literary excellence. The Central Government honoured him with the Padma Shri award. Wrote short stories, novels, travelogues, criticism, biographies etc. Penned more than fifty books belonging to different genres. He also worked as the President of the Odisha Sahitya Akademi and editor as well as

Chief Editor of The Sambad, a local daily in Odisha. *Mahanagarira Ratri, Maralara Mrutyu, Andha Diganta, Mahanirvana* are his significant contributions. His novels *Nilasaila, Niladri Vijaya, Krushnavenire Sandhya* are based on history, myth and legends.

Kishori Charan Das (1924-2018): An eminent bilingual writer who wrote both in Odia and English. He was a poet, novelist, short story writer and essayist. Awarded with the Odisha Sahitya Akademi , Sarala Puraskar, Bishuva Puraskar besides others. He is a master story teller dealing with the insecurities and uncertainties of the middle class. His stories present 'the realities of everyday life in a straightforward manner and unassuming style'. Some of his notable contributions include *Bhanga Khelana, Ghara Bahuda, Manihara, Thakura Ghara, Bhinna Paunsha*, The Midnight Moon and Other Stories etc.

Achyutananda Pati (b 1926): Odisha Sahitya Akademi award winner for his short story collection *Snayu O Sanyasi*. Also has been awarded with The Atibadi Jagannath Das award, the highest literary award of the Odisha Sahitya Akademi. Started his literary career in 1952. However, he established himself in the late 1960's. *Asubha Putrara kahani, Ugrasen Ubacha* and *Nia Jaluchhi* are among his best collection of stories. His compassion for the poor and the down trodden get reflected in his stories.

Mohapatra Nilamani Sahoo (1926-2016): Reputed to be a writer of short stories, novels, one-act plays, children's plays and an editor. Received awards like the Odia Sahitya Akademi award, the Central Sahitya Akademi award, Sarala award, Sahitya Bharati award among others. Edited The Jhankar, The Utkal Prasanga and The Odisha Review. His popular works include *Prema Tribhuja, Michha Bagha, Ganjei O' Gabeshana, Akasha Patala, Abhisapta Gandharba* etc.

Akhila Mohan Pattnaik (1927-1987): A popular short story writer in Odia. Honoured with the Central Sahitya Akademi award for his *O' Andhagali*. Was influenced by leftist ideology. Among his popular collection of stories popular are *O' Andhagali, Jhadara Eagle O Dharanira Krushnasara, Nadira nama Ganatantra, Pratham O' Sesha* etc.

Chandrasekhar Rath (1929-2018): Awarded with the Central Sahitya Akademi, Odisha Sahitya Akademi, Sahitya Bharati, Sarala Puraskar, The Atibadi Jagannath Das award and Padma Shri, Chandrasekhar Rath was a short story writer, novelist, sculptor, painter, poet, essayist, and critic in Odia. He is credited to have written three novels, fourteen collections of short stories, twelve collections of essays besides others. His remarkable contributions include *Yantrarudha, Asurya Upanibesh, Nabajataka, Anek Banya Pare, Awsarohira Galpa, Samrat O Anyamane, Anya Eka Sakala, Sabutharu Dirgha Rati* etc.

Manoj Das (1934-2021): The Padma Shri and Padma Bhusan awarded internationally acclaimed bilingual writer writing in Odia and English. Won the Central Sahitya Akademi award in 1972 for his story collection *Manoj Dasanka Katha O Kahani*. Received the Odia Sahitya Akademi award for his essay-criticism titled Kete Diganta. Also honoured with the Atibadi Jagannath Das award, the highest literary award of the Odisha Sahitya Akademi. Started his career in the post-independence period. Humane attitude, novelty in selection of and treatment of subject matter, blending of intellect and satire, and a keen observation of social relationships lent newness to his stories. Kings, emperors, Zamindars as well as saints and nobles are often the characters in his stories. Collections like *Samudra Kshudha, Jibanara Swada, Bisakanyara Kahani, Manoj Dasanka Katha O Kahani* have immortalized him.

Rabi Pattanayak (1935-1991): Honoured with the Central Sahitya Akademi award, Odisha Sahitya Akademi award and Sarala award for his contributions to literature. His significant contributions include *Raga Todi, Bahurupi, Vichitravarna, Prema O Pratima, Andhagalira Andhakar, Megha Malhara, Abinasvara* etc.

Binapani Mohanty (b1936): Central Sahitya Akademi award winning writer. Awarded in 1990 for her work Patadei. Received the Odisha Sahitya Akademi award for her short story collection *Kasturi Mruga O Sabuja Aranya*. Also awarded with the Atibadi Jagannath Das award, the highest literary award of the Odisha Sahitya Akademi. She is well-known for the large number of stories written on feminine psychology. Torture of women, the staggering position of women in the family, the various problems that women encounter in their day-to-day life find place in her stories. The stories are full of pathos and sorrow. Most of her characters are rebels who refuse to accept things lying down. *Nabataranga, Kasturimruga O sabuja Aranya, Kalantara, Arohan* are among her best collections.

Pratibha Ray (b 1944): Winner of the Bharatiya Jnanapitha award, Ray is the only female Moortidevi Award winner. She has immensely enriched the modern Odia literature by her pioneering short stories and novels. Awarded with the Central Sahitya Akademi award for her collection of stories *Ullanghana*, her notable collection of stories include *Ketakibana, Pratibha Katha Kalpa, Radhara Banshi, Saila sayini, Hatabaksa* etc. Her stories reflect the spirit of the times, the nuances of feminine psychology, desire for social reforms, compassion for fellow beings, propagation of Odishan culture etc. Her works not only reflect the urban milieu but also delve deeply into tribal life and customs. She is also the recipient of the Odisha Sahitya Akademi award, Padma Shri, Amrita Keerti Puraskar etc.

Ramachandra Behera (b 1945): Atibadi Jagannath Das and Sarala Puraskar winner. A compassionate writer, he writes about the present world and the other world. On one hand, he has the life of man which is ridden with troubles and poverty. Man finds himself helpless and aloof. On the other hand, there is his mind and the spiritual world whose workings are not known. Both life and the world are incomplete. His stories delineate the struggle of the characters to overcome the difficulties and register victory. *Dwitiya Smasan, Achinha Pruthibi, Abasistha Ayusha* are his famous collections. Won the Central Sahitya Akademi award in 2005 for his collection of stories *Gopapura*.

Tarun Kanti Mishra (b 1950): Central Sahitya Akademi award winner-2019 for his work *Bhaswati*. Has also been awarded with the Odisha Sahitya Akademi award and Sarala award for invaluable contributions to literature. Written more than three hundred stories in twenty-one anthologies. In his stories, he delves deep into the fathomless sea of life and brings to the fore its secrets. He has written many stories on 'hunger, deprivation, opulence and hypocrisy of modern times'. *Komala Gandhara, Nisangatara Swara, Bahubrihi, Prajapatira Dena nahi, Ajana Tithira janha, Aji Ratira Galpa* are some of his notable works.

Gourahari Das (b 1960): A Central Sahitya Akademi and Odisha Sahitya Akademi award winning writer. He is a novelist, short story writer, dramatist, columnist, journalist, editor, translator-- all blended into one. A writer of more than sixty books, he has five novels, thirteen collections of short stories, more than five hundred vignettes written over a span of thirty years, three plays besides others. The experience that he deals with in his stories is never outlandish. The characters are all very common and can be found everywhere. The readers can relate to his stories. *Akhadaghara, Bharatvarsha, Matikandhei, Ghara, Bidesh O Anyanya galpa, Chhaya soudhara Abashesha, Nija Sange Nijara Ladhei* are some of his notable works.

Black Eagle Books

www.blackeaglebooks.org
info@blackeaglebooks.org

Black Eagle Books, an independent publisher, was founded
as a nonprofit organization in April, 2019. It is our mission
to connect and engage the Indian diaspora and the world at
large with the best of works of world literature published
on a collaborative platform, with special emphasis on
foregrounding Contemporary Classics and New Writing.